Dante's Purgatory: A Retelling in Prose

David Bruce

Published by David Bruce, 2022.

This is a work of fiction. Similarities to real people, places, or events are entirely coincidental.

DANTE'S PURGATORY: A RETELLING IN PROSE

First edition. July 5, 2022.

Copyright © 2022 David Bruce.

ISBN: 979-8201608170

Written by David Bruce.

Table of Contents

Dedication

Dedicated to Carl Eugene Bruce and Josephine Saturday Bruce

My father, Carl Eugene Bruce, died on 24 October 2013. He used to work for Ohio Power, and at one time, his job was to shut off the electricity of people who had not paid their bills. He sometimes would find a home with an impoverished mother and some children. Instead of shutting off their electricity, he would tell the mother that she needed to pay her bill or soon her electricity would be shut off. He would write on a form that no one was home when he stopped by because if no one was home he did not have to shut off their electricity.

The best good deed that anyone ever did for my father occurred after a storm that knocked down many power lines. He and other linemen worked long hours and got wet and cold. Their feet were freezing because water got into their boots and soaked their socks. Fortunately, a kind woman gave my father and the other linemen dry socks to wear.

My mother, Josephine Saturday Bruce, died on 14 June 2003. She used to work at a store that sold clothing. One day, an impoverished mother with a baby clothed in rags walked into the store and started shoplifting in an interesting way: The mother took the rags off her baby and dressed the infant in new clothing. My mother knew that this mother could not afford to buy the clothing, but she helped the mother dress her baby and then she watched as the mother walked out of the store without paying.

***

The doing of good deeds is important. As a free person, you can choose to live your life as a good person or as a bad person. To be a good person, do good deeds. To be a bad person, do bad deeds. If you do good deeds, you will become good. If you do bad deeds, you will become bad. To become the person you want to be, act as if you already are that kind of person. Each of us chooses what kind of person we will become. To become a good person, do the things a good person does. To become a bad person, do the things a bad person does. The opportunity to take action to become the kind of person you want to be is yours.

Human beings have free will. According to the Babylonian Niddah 16b, whenever a baby is to be conceived, the Lailah (angel in charge of contraception) takes the drop of semen that will result in the conception and asks God, "Sovereign of the Universe, what is going to be the fate of this drop? Will it develop into a robust or into a weak person? An intelligent or a stupid person? A wealthy or a poor person?" The Lailah asks all these questions, but it does not ask, "Will it develop into a righteous or a wicked person?" The answer to that question lies in the decisions to be freely made by the human being that is the result of the conception.

A Buddhist monk visiting a class wrote this on the chalkboard: "EVERYONE WANTS TO SAVE THE WORLD, BUT NO ONE WANTS TO HELP MOM DO THE DISHES." The students laughed, but the monk then said, "Statistically, it's highly unlikely that any of you will ever have the opportunity to run into a burning orphanage and rescue an infant. But, in the smallest gesture of kindness — a warm smile, holding the door for the person behind you, shoveling the driveway of the elderly person next door — you have committed an act of immeasurable profundity, because to each of us, our life is our universe."

Educate Yourself
Read Like A Wolf Eats
Be Excellent to Each Other
Books Then, Books Now, Books Forever

In this retelling, as in all my retellings, I have tried to make the work of literature accessible to modern readers who may lack the knowledge about mythology, religion, and history that the literary work's contemporary audience had.

Do you know a language other than English? If you do, I give you permission to translate this book, copyright your translation, publish or self-publish it, and keep all the royalties for yourself. (Do give me credit, of course, for the original retelling.)

I would like to see my retellings of classic literature used in schools, so I give permission to the country of Finland (and all other countries) to give copies of any or all of my retellings to all students forever. I also give permission to the state of Texas (and all other states) to give copies of any or all of my retellings to all students forever. I also give permission to all teachers to give copies of any or all of my retellings to all students forever. Of course, libraries are welcome to use my eBooks for free.

Teachers need not actually teach my retellings. Teachers are welcome to give students copies of my eBooks as background material. For example, if they are teaching Homer's *Iliad* and *Odyssey*, teachers are welcome to give students copies of my *Virgil's* Aeneid: *A Retelling in Prose* and tell them, "Here's another ancient epic you may want to read in your spare time."

Note: Two characters in this book are Dante the Pilgrim and Dante the Poet. Dante the Pilgrim is the character who is climbing up the Mountain of Purgatory. Dante the Poet is the same character, but older and wiser. Dante the Poet has visited the Inferno, Purgatory, and Paradise and has much more knowledge than Dante the Pilgrim.

PURGATORY

Chapter 1: The Island of Purgatory and Cato the Guard (Purgatory)

Dante the Poet thought, *Now my talent for poetry must be put to a new test. I have left behind me the Inferno, where unrepentant sinners are punished. Now my subject is Purgatory, where repentant sinners are purged of their sins so that they may ascend to Paradise. Muses, let my poetry be worthy of this subject! Let Calliope, the Muse of Epic Poetry and the leader of the other Muses, assist me! Let Calliope keep me from pride! Pride would keep me from telling this part of my tale correctly. Once, the proud daughters of King Pierus, whom he had named after you Muses, challenged you Muses to a contest of song. They had unwisely sung a song about the proud giants known as the Titans rebelling against their rightful ruler, Jupiter, King of the gods. You, Calliope, sang a song that utterly defeated the proud daughters of King Pierus, and then you changed them into magpies. They were proud challengers, but I am a humble suppliant. Pride is the worst and the foundation of all sins. Please, Calliope, sing for my benefit so that I may properly write about the Mountain of Purgatory!*

Dante the Pilgrim looked around him at the base of the Mountain of Purgatory. He and his guide, Virgil, had entered the Inferno on Good Friday of the year 1300. Now, on Easter Sunday, 10 April 1300, dawn was nearing. The Inferno is always in darkness, but here on the Mountain of Purgatory are both day and night. The air of the Inferno always stank, but here the air is always pleasing. Sinners of the Inferno never saw Venus, the planet of love, but here Dante looked up at the sky and saw the bright and beautiful planet.

Dante the Pilgrim then looked to his right, and he saw four stars.

Dante the Poet thought, *These are the stars that the first man, Adam, saw clearly, and no man since him has ever seen so clearly. These four stars, which can be clearly seen from the Forest of Eden, are Prudence, Temperance, Justice, and Fortitude. They are the four cardinal virtues. A person who has Prudence is able to judge which of a number of actions is the correct action to pursue. A person who has Temperance is able to practice self-control when self-control is needed. A person who has Justice is able to correctly balance his or her own self-interest with the needs of* others, and a person who has Courage is able to conquer fear so that he or she can do the right thing. Virtuous pagans such as Virgil have the cardinal virtues.

Dante looked away from the four stars, and he saw an old man of dignity who commanded respect. Any stranger looking at him felt like a good son looking at a good father. The old man was alone. His beard was long, and it was streaked with white among the black. His hair was long, and on each side of his head his hair flowed down to his chest. His face was brightly lit with rays from the four stars. In fact, so brightly lit was it that a viewer could almost say that the Sun — given to us by God — was shining on the old man's face.

The old man saw Dante and Virgil and asked, "Who are you? You have escaped from the Inferno by climbing along the passage through which a stream flows from the Forest of Eden at the top of the Mountain of Purgatory into Cocytus in the Inferno. Who is your guide? Who provided you with light to escape from the forever-dark pit of Hell? Have the laws of God changed? Has God decided that some of the damned may come to the Mountain of Purgatory?"

Dante thought, This is interesting. Can God change His laws? Why not? Once we had an Old Testament and now we have a New Testament. God is all-powerful, all-knowing, and all-good. God is not limited. Could God decree that a virtuous pagan enter Paradise? Why not? God is all-powerful. God is not limited by Humankind's interpretation of the Bible. If God were to allow virtuous pagans into Paradise, it would be a triumph for Omnipotent Love.

Virgil had recognized the old man. Virgil grabbed Dante's arm, and motioned for him to kneel and show respect to the old man. Dante quickly obeyed.

Virgil thought, This man is Cato the Younger. He is also known as Cato the Stoic and as Cato of Utica. In his life, he was renowned for possessing Prudence, Temperance, Justice, and Courage in abundance. He was morally upright. He understood law. He valued freedom. He declined to take bribes. He detested the corruption of his age. When war broke out between Julius Caesar and Pompey the Great, Cato sided with Pompey because he believed that Julius Caesar was the greater enemy of freedom. When Julius Caesar decisively defeated Pompey at Utica, Cato committed suicide there rather than submit to a person whom he considered to be a foe of freedom. Such a suicide is much different from that of Pier della Vigne, who committed suicide out of self-pity and the hope of getting people

Virgil spoke to Cato, "I am not here to help myself. I am here on a mission given to me from a lady in Paradise. She asked me to be a guide for this man. You have requested that we explain what we are doing here, and I will obey your request. This man is still alive; he has not yet died. To avoid being condemned to the Inferno after he dies, he needs help, and so a lady in Paradise asked me to help him. This is the only way that he can avoid eternal damnation. I have guided him through the Inferno with all its damned souls, and now I need to show him all those who are on the Mountain of Purgatory to get him ready to enter Paradise. It is the will of Heaven that we proceed. Please welcome this man. He is searching for freedom, and you value freedom so highly. You committed suicide at Utica because you loved freedom so much. There you cast off your body — a body with which you will be reunited on the Great Day that is the Day of Judgment. Neither this man nor I have broken Heaven's laws by coming here. This man is still alive, and Minos has never judged me and found me guilty. I come from Limbo, where the virtuous pagans, including Marcia, your wife, resides. Marcia loves you and still wishes to be your wife. Out of your love of her, please allow us to climb the seven ledges of the Mountain of Purgatory. I will tell her of your kindness to us, if you will allow me to mention your name in Limbo."

Cato said, "While I was alive, I would do anything for Marcia. But now I am doing the Will of a Greater Power, and she can no longer command me. But since a Heavenly lady wishes you to be here and to climb the mountain, that is all that is necessary. You may climb the mountain. You need not flatter me. Take this man and tie a humble reed around his waist. Also clean his face. The tears of Hell are on his face, and it is not fitting that he see angels. Go down to where the waves break upon the shore. Reeds are growing in soft sand. Most plants cannot survive there; the waves would break their stalks. But the humble reed bows before the waves and so survives. When you are ready to climb the mountain, do not come back here. The daylight will show you where to go."

Cato left them.

Dante rose from his knees, and he looked at Virgil.

Virgil said to him, "Follow me. I see where the reeds grow."

Daylight was more pronounced, and Dante could see the waves. Dante and Virgil walked to the shore. They were like two men who had wandered from a path and were eager to find the path again.

They reached a place that was still shaded, and so the dew remained. Virgil put his hands in the dewy grass, and Dante turned his face to him. Virgil cleaned from Dante's face the traces of the tears that he had shed when he had pitied some sinners in the Inferno — a pity that had angered Virgil and that Dante had learned was undeserved. Once again, Dante had a clean face with no trace of Hell left on it.

Then Virgil pulled a reed to tie around Dante's waist. Immediately, another reed grew to take its place.

This is a place of miracles, Dante thought. *It is also a place of growth. Good things happen here.*

Chapter 2: New Souls Arrive in Purgatory (Purgatory)

Dawn arrived, and Dante and Virgil looked around them, wondering in which direction they should go. Then Dante saw far out at sea on the horizon a light like that of Mars as it glows through fog.

Dante the Poet thought, *That is a light that I would like to see again!*

The light moved quickly. Dante the Pilgrim looked at Virgil and then looked out at sea again. The light was brighter and much closer than before. Two spots of whiteness appeared beside the light, and then a spot of whiteness appeared under the light, and Virgil, recognizing now what he was seeing, told Dante, "Fall to your knees! Look! The angel of the Lord is coming! Fold your hands! You will see more angels like him!"

Dante looked, and now he saw that the two spots of whiteness on either side of the light were the wings of the angel and the spot of brightness under the light was the body of the angel.

Virgil said, "See how the angel scorns to use any human-made means of acceleration! The angel does not need oars or sails! Only the movement of the angel's wings powers the boat! See how the angel has the wings pointed toward Heaven! The wings have feathers that do not molt as do the feathers of birds on earth!"

The angel came closer and closer to the Island of Purgatory, and as he came closer and closer, he shone brighter and brighter until Dante could no longer look at him and had to bow his head.

The angel steered straight to the shore on his swift and light boat, on which over 100 souls were on board. All the souls were singing "*In Exitu Israel de Aegypto*" — "When Israel Came Out of Egypt." This song is Psalm 114, of which these souls, who were leaving exile to go to Paradise, sang every verse:

"When Israel went out of Egypt, the house of Jacob from a people of strange language;

"Judah was his sanctuary, and Israel his dominion.

"The sea saw it, and fled: Jordan was driven back.

"The mountains skipped like rams, and the little hills like lambs.

"What ailed you, O sea, that you fled? You, Jordan, that you were driven back?

"You, mountains, that you skipped like rams; and you, little hills, like lambs?

"Tremble, you earth, at the presence of the Lord, at the presence of the God of Jacob;

"Who turned the rock into a standing water, the flint into a fountain of waters."

Dante thought, *This is a place of song, unlike the Inferno. And this is a place where people come to end their exile from God, also unlike the Inferno.*

The angel made the sign of the cross, allowed the souls to disembark from the boat, and then left as quickly as he had come.

The newly arrived souls curiously examined their surroundings; after all, they were strangers to this place. Full morning had arrived, and one of the newly arrived souls shouted to Dante and Virgil, "Do you know where is the road that leads up the mountain? If you do, please show it to us."

Virgil replied, "We are not yet familiar with this place. We are like you, newly arrived, but we came here by way of a journey that will make climbing up the mountain seem easy."

Dante thought, *This is a place where one can ask for help, and no doubt, usually get it. We asked Cato for help, and he willingly gave it to us. If Virgil and I had the knowledge that would answer these souls' questions, we would willingly share our knowledge with them. In the Inferno, souls seldom ask for help, and seldom do they get help. And when they do get help or pity, it is from a naïve visitor such as me.*

Then the newly arrived souls noticed something odd about Dante: He breathed! He was still alive! The souls crowded around Dante, curious about him and forgetting the reason they were on the Island of Purgatory: to climb the Mountain of Purgatory so that they could see God.

One soul in particular was happy to see Dante. This soul came toward Dante with arms outstretched as if he wanted to hug him. Dante did not recognize this soul, but willing to be gracious in such a place, he came toward the soul and attempted three times to embrace him, but each time he failed.

Virgil thought, *This is like the scene in Homer's* Odyssey *in which Odysseus visits the Underworld and sees his mother. Three times he tries to embrace her, but he fails each time. His living body is unable to touch her soul. This is also like two scenes in my* Aeneid. *In fleeing Troy, Aeneas' wife, Creusa, dies. Aeneas returns to the city to find and rescue her, but he sees her shade. Three times he tries to embrace her, but each time he fails. Later, Aeneas is in the Underworld, where he sees the shade of his late father, Anchises. Three times he tries to embrace him, but each time he fails.*

Dante was surprised, but the soul smiled and suggested that he not try again to embrace him.

Now Dante knew the identity of the soul by the richness of his voice. This was the soul of his friend Casella, who had died months ago and who was a singer, a musician, and a poet. Dante begged him to stay and talk.

Casella replied, "We were friends when I was alive, and we are still friends although I am dead. Of course, I will stay and talk to you. But why are you, a living man, here now?"

Dante said, "I am making this journey as a living man now in hopes that I will be worthy to come back here after I am dead rather than being condemned to the Inferno. But you died months ago. Why has it taken you so long to arrive here?"

Casella replied, "I have no complaint. The angel often declined to take me on board his boat, for God, who is always just, guides the angel's will. But three months ago, Pope Boniface VIII granted a plenary indulgence because 1300 is the great Jubilee Year, a time of joy, of pardon, of remission of the punishment of sin. We saved souls have been forgiven our sins, but we still must go through Purgatory so that we become purged of all sin. God does not always allow those who have died to come quickly to the Mountain of Purgatory. If we kept God waiting until we became Christians late in life, God keeps us waiting at the mouth of the Tiber River, where the saved souls assemble. By granting a plenary indulgence, Pope Boniface VIII allowed those of us who kept God waiting by becoming Christians late in life the chance to come quicker to the Mountain of Purgatory than we otherwise would. Because of the plenary indulgence, all any of us have to do is to ask the angel to take us here, and the angel will do it. Even now, the angel is heading back to the Tiber to pick up another load of saved souls."

Dante thought, *Pope Boniface VIII is doomed to the Inferno, but even he can do a good deed sometimes. God can accomplish much even through the deeds of evil men. And what about you, Casella? For three months, all you had to do was ask the angel to bring you here and he would have done it, but only now are you arriving here. Did you do a good deed by allowing others to arrive here first? Or did you feel not worthy yet to come here?*

Dante asked, "If no law forbids it, I would like to hear a love song, one of those that brought me happiness on Earth. Please sing one, and help me to rid myself of some of the exhaustion I have suffered as a result of my journey."

Casella was willing, and he began singing, "*Amor Che Ne la Mente Mi Ragiona*," or "Love, that Within My Mind Discourses with Me."

Dante thought, *I wrote the poem that Casella is singing. Casella set it to music.*

Dante, Virgil, and all the newly arrived souls listened to the line with great enjoyment, but their enjoyment was quickly interrupted.

Cato, the Just Old Man, appeared and shouted, "WHAT ARE YOU DOING? YOU NEED TO CONCENTRATE ON YOUR SOULS, NOT ON SILLY LOVE SONGS! KEEP YOUR EYES ON THE PRIZE! RUN TO THE MOUNTAIN! LOOK FOR THE PLACE AND THE TIME TO BEGIN CLIMBING!"

You may have seen a flock of pigeons feeding in a field and strutting, showing off their fine feathers. But they are suddenly interrupted and instantly fly away.

Like the pigeons, the newly arrived souls instantly fled — and so did Dante and Virgil.

Dante thought, *So this is the job of Cato — to make sure that the saved souls stay focused on the job of purging their sins. Obviously, these souls are not yet perfected, just as Virgil and I are not. Obviously, they — as well as Virgil and I — can be distracted from the job they and we ought to be doing.*

Chapter 3: Prepurgatory — The Excommunicated (Purgatory)

The recently arrived souls raced ahead, but Dante stayed close to Virgil, who slowed down and felt remorse.

Virgil thought, *My job is to be Dante's guide and to make sure that he sees what is necessary to save his soul, but here I have failed. I should have known that secular love songs are not permitted here because the purpose of Purgatory is to prepare souls to enter Paradise.*

Striding beside Virgil, who had resumed his normal pace, and heading west, Dante looked up at the mountain in front of him. But as he raised his eyes, he noticed his shadow. He also noticed that only one shadow — his own — was ahead of him. Afraid that Virgil might have abandoned him, he looked quickly beside him.

Virgil noticed and said, "Why are you worried? Did you think that I am not still your guide? Are you surprised that I have no shadow? Your body blocks the Sun's rays, but my body lies in the tomb in Naples to which it was taken by the order of Caesar Augustus after my body had been buried in Brindisi, where I died. Because I have no body, I do not cast a shadow. But although I have no body, I can still feel pain and feel cold and feel heat, all by the order of God, whose Will cannot be totally known by us humans. None of us outside of Paradise will ever be able to understand the Trinity: Three Persons in One Being. Be satisfied with knowing the Fact of some things without knowing the Why. If we humans knew everything, Mary need not have given birth to Jesus. You have visited Limbo. There people such as Plato and Aristotle and others reside who would like to know the Why but never will. Such souls know that they will never reach Paradise and acquire such understanding. Because of this, they suffer endless pain."

Virgil was silent and unhappy.

Dante thought, *Virgil is thinking that he is one of those who reside in Limbo and will never reach Paradise.*

Dante and Virgil reached the foot of the mountain. Looking at its side, they saw that it was so steep and so sheer that they had no chance of climbing it. Any of the mountains in any of the other parts of the Earth would be an easy climb compared to this.

Virgil asked himself and Dante, "How can we find a place at which we can begin to scale this mountain?"

Virgil's head bent low as he thought, and Dante's head raised high as he looked at the mountain. A crowd of souls came toward them from their left — a crowd of souls moving so slowly that they seemed not to be moving.

Dante said to Virgil, "Look over there! Some people are coming who should be able to help us find a way up this mountain — if you have not already thought of a way."

Virgil looked, and relieved, he said, "Let us go to meet them because they are moving so slowly, and you, you continue to hope that they can help us."

Dante and Virgil walked a thousand steps toward the group of souls and were as far away from them as a person who is talented with a slingshot could throw a stone. Then the group of souls halted and stared at them.

Virgil said, "Saved souls, you ended your lives well, with the promise of eventually residing in Paradise. Please tell us in which place the mountain is not so steep that it cannot be climbed. We are eager to climb it, and we regret the time that we spend waiting."

One of the saved souls moved forward, and then another, and then another, until the entire group was moving forward, slowly. Dante thought, *They look like a group of sheep that lack a shepherd. Sheep move like that. One or two move, and then the others follow them. The sheep move so slowly because they have no shepherd to keep them moving.*

But the saved souls in front saw Dante's shadow. They stopped and backed up. The saved souls in the back also backed up, although they did not know the reason for backing up.

Virgil said, "I know what is bothering you. This man casts a shadow because he is still living. But do not be afraid. This man would not be here if it were not the will of Heaven. His purpose for being here is to climb the mountain."

The saved souls replied, "Go ahead of us in the direction in which we are heading. You will find the place from which you may climb the mountain."

One of the saved souls in front said, "As you walk forward in pursuit of your goal — I don't want to keep you from accomplishing your purpose — look backward at me and see if you recognize me."

Dante looked back and looked closely at the saved soul, who was blond and looked like a patrician, although a sword had cut through one of his eyebrows.

Although Dante looked closely at the saved soul, he had to confess that he did not recognize him.

The saved soul then showed Dante a gash above his breast — a second mortal wound. The saved soul smiled and said, "I am Manfred. My grandmother is the Empress Constance. I humbly request that when you are again in the Land of the Living, go and see my daughter, whose sons are the King of Aragon and the King of Sicily. No doubt, rumors are that I was sentenced to spend eternity in the Inferno because I was excommunicated. Tell my daughter that as I lay dying with these two mortal wounds, I was saved. I asked forgiveness for my sins from God. My sins were horrible, but God's forgiveness is infinite. All who believe that their sins are incapable of being forgiven by God are guilty of the sin of pride."

Dante thought, *Why is Manfred smiling as he says these words? He may simply be amused that I do not recognize him. Manfred was famous. I have heard of him although I did not recognize him, Manfred is humble; he did not get angry when I failed to recognize him. Manfred was killed in the Battle of Benevento in 1266, the battle that led to the return of the Guelfs to Florence — I was one year old at the time. Or Manfred could be smiling because I will be able to give the good news of his salvation to his daughter. He is happy that I can give good news to his daughter and make her happy. His daughter will know that he is a saved soul and is not suffering the torments of Hell. Or perhaps Manfred is smiling because he is aware that I am likely to think that he does not belong here in Purgatory. He may be thinking, I bet you didn't think I was saved, did you? After all, I know that he was excommunicated. But it does not take years of penance to get God's mercy. All it takes is a moment, and Manfred repented his sins in the very last moment of his life.*

Manfred continued, "Because I was excommunicated from the Church, my bones were dug up by the Pastor of Cosenza who was following the orders of Pope Clement IV. The Pastor of Cosenza then cast my bones outside Church territory. Now the wind and the rain buffet my bones. But even though I was excommunicated, that will not keep me from Paradise. Repentance and salvation can occur in the very last moment of life."

Dante thought, *Manfred is right. Excommunication is being expelled formally from a religious body. Excommunication is not the same thing as damnation. God decides where we will go in the afterlife, not the Church. I see that Manfred is not angry about how his body was treated on Earth. Many sinners in the Inferno were angry. Manfred is happy that he was saved.*

Excommunication does mean being without a shepherd. Manfred and other excommunicated souls did not have a shepherd to guide them because they were separated from the Church.

Manfred continued, "But those who are excommunicated, although they repent at the end of life, must stay at the foot of the mountain for thirty times as long as they were excommunicated. However, prayers by the living for the dead can shorten that time. Please tell my daughter that. I hope that she will pray for me and others."

Dante thought, *Manfred is a saved soul, but his father, the Holy Roman Emperor Frederick II, is in the Inferno — he is in the tomb with Farinata. Members of the same family can end up in different places in the afterlife.*

Chapter 4: Prepurgatory — The Spiritually Lazy (Purgatory)

Dante was so interested in what Manfred had to say that he had lost track of time. Suddenly aware that much time had passed, he thought, *A human being has only one soul, although it may have more than one part. If he or she had two or more souls, one soul would be able to pay particular attention to what Manfred had to say while another soul would be able to pay particular attention to the passage of time. He is wrong who teaches that human beings have more than one soul. The Christian theologian Thomas Aquinas was correct when he stated that a human being has one unified soul with three parts.*

The souls with whom Dante and Virgil were traveling called out, "Here is the way up the mountain that you have been searching for." Dante and Virgil began climbing, while the souls continued their journey.

The gap was narrow, and it was steep, and climbing it required the use of both hands and both feet. Think of San Leo and Noli. Those towns are on steep hills that you can climb with your feet only, but this mountain cannot be climbed so easily.

Dante and Virgil climbed up the narrow passageway. They rested briefly, and Dante asked, "Where do we now go?" Virgil replied, "Straight up, as we have been going. We must not be distracted. We must find an experienced person to guide us for a while."

They climbed, but Dante grew exhausted. He pleaded to Virgil, "Listen to me, please. I must stop. I cannot keep up with you."

Virgil replied, "Keep climbing until we reach the open area that we can see from here. Then you can rest."

They climbed and reached the open area and rested. They looked down at the area that they had traveled. Seeing the distance that a traveler had already traveled can put heart in a tired traveler.

Dante looked at the shore, which was far below him, and then he looked up at the Sun, but it was not where he expected it to be. Virgil, who knew Dante's thoughts and his questions, said, "The Sun is not where you expected it to be because you are in the Southern Hemisphere. You are no longer in Italy, which is in the Northern Hemisphere. Think of a person high in the Northern

Hemisphere looking at the equator. That person will see the Sun travel from left to right. Now imagine a person low in the Southern Hemisphere looking at the equator. That person will see the Sun travel from right to left."

Dante said, "I understand, but can you tell me now how much more climbing we have to do? We have done much steep and difficult climbing, but still the peak of the mountain is so high that I cannot see it."

Virgil replied, "This mountain is different from other mountains. This mountain is the most difficult of all mountains to climb, but it is hardest at the beginning of the climb. The higher one climbs, the easier the climbing becomes. When climbing the mountain becomes as easy as floating in a boat down a river, then you have reached the end of your journey."

Dante thought, *Resisting sin is like climbing this mountain. Turning away from sin is very difficult at first, but it becomes easier as one's will grows stronger. As one's will is strengthened and perfected, it becomes much easier to resist sin. In other words, the higher one climbs up the mountain, the more one purges his or her sin. The more sin one purges, the easier it is to climb up the mountain.*

Dante and Virgil then heard a voice: "Before you ... reach the top ... of this mountain ... you will feel ... like resting."

Dante and Virgil turned in the direction from which the voice had come. They saw a boulder that they had not looked closely at, and they saw some souls resting in its shade.

All of the souls looked tired — or lazy. One soul was sitting with his arms wrapped around his knees and his head drooping between his legs.

Dante said to Virgil, "Look at this soul! No man on Earth could look more like a lazy man, not even if his middle name were 'Lazy.'"

The lazy soul barely lifted his head and looked at Dante and said, "If ... unlike me ... you are filled ... with energy ... run up ... this mountain."

Dante recognized the soul by his voice. Still exhausted from his climb, Dante staggered toward him.

The lazy soul teased Dante: "Do you now know ... why the Sun ... travels from your right ... to your left?"

Dante half-smiled and said to the soul whom he now recognized to be a friend, one who in the Land of the Living made parts for musical instruments when he could rouse himself from laziness, "Belacqua, now I need not worry about what happened to you after your death! You are a saved soul, and you will see Paradise! But why are you sitting here? Are you waiting for a guide? Or are you as lazy here as you were in the Land of the Living?"

Dante thought, *The unrepentant slothful are punished in the Inferno, and I was afraid that my friend Belacqua would be punished there. But any sin can be forgiven if it is sincerely repented.*

Belacqua replied, "Climbing will not do me ... any good ... just yet. ... The angel ... will not allow me to pass ... from Prepurgatory ... into Purgatory Proper ... until as many years ... pass here ... as passed ... until I repented ... at the very end ... of my life. ... I kept God waiting ... and now ... as is proper ... God keeps me ... waiting. ... However ... God is merciful ... and if ... people pray for me ... I may go ... to Purgatory Proper ... and start climbing ... the Mountain of Purgatory ... sooner ... as long as ... the prayers come ... from a good heart. ... The prayers ... of evil people ... such as hypocrites ... are not heard ... in Heaven."

Dante thought, *I see what is going on in Prepurgatory. Here are the souls who are waiting to climb the Mountain of Purgatory. They made God wait — by waiting to repent — and so God is making them wait to climb the mountain. Virgil and I have already seen the excommunicated and the slothful. Perhaps we will see other kinds of late-repentant souls.*

Virgil said to Dante, "It is already noon," and then Virgil started climbing the mountain again.

Chapter 5: Prepurgatory — Those Who Repented While Meeting Violent, Sudden Deaths (Purgatory)

Dante had turned to follow Virgil, when one of the spiritually lazy souls said, "Look! He is casting a shadow! He seems to be still alive!"

Dante turned around and saw the souls staring at him and his shadow.

Virgil turned around and asked Dante, "What has distracted your attention now? Focus on your real reason for being here. Do not care if the souls here whisper about you. Follow me and let me lead you upward. Be like a stone tower that resists the winds. Don't be like a man whose attention is easily distracted from what is important."

Virgil thought, *I can see why Cato is needed here. Too often, souls here — even myself earlier — allow themselves to be distracted. Cato is needed to remind these souls to keep their eyes on the prize.*

Dante, shamed and blushing, said, "I am coming now."

Another group of souls was coming and chanting the *Miserere*, a Psalm asking for the forgiveness of sins. Some souls sang one part, and the other souls sang another part, alternating parts until all the lines of the Psalm had been sung. The first lines they sang were these:

"Have mercy upon me, O God, according to Your lovingkindness: according to the multitude of Your tender mercies blot out my transgressions.

"Wash me thoroughly from my iniquity, and cleanse me from my sin.

"For I acknowledge my transgressions: and my sin is ever before me."

Dante thought, *Music is a part of at least Prepurgatory. It may also be a part of Purgatory Proper and maybe even beyond. Music is not a part of the Inferno. Music and the Psalms are an important part of the life of monks. Preparing for Purgatory can be started while one is still alive on Earth. The monks do that.*

This group of souls also noticed that Dante was casting a shadow, and two of this group of souls came running toward Dante. These souls asked, "Who are you? Please tell us your stories."

Virgil replied, "You may return and tell the other souls that this man beside me is still alive. I know that they must be surprised because he is casting a shadow. These souls may profit from becoming acquainted with him."

The two souls ran back to the other souls, and all the souls came running up to Dante and Virgil.

Virgil said, "Many souls are coming toward us. Each will want a favor from you. Listen to them, but keep walking as you listen."

The souls asked Dante, "You, who are still alive, please look at us and see if you recognize any of us. If you do, please bring back news of that person to those still living. Please stop and listen to us. All of us met a violent death, and all of us repented in our last moments of life. When we died, we were at peace with God. We left life longing to see God."

Dante replied, "I clearly see your faces, but I do not recognize any of you saved souls. But if I can do something to help you, please tell me, and I will help you."

One of the souls said, "We know that you will keep your word unless you are prevented by some powerful reason. I will make my plea first. If you ever go to the town of Fano, please tell the souls there to pray for me so I may sooner begin my journey through Purgatory Proper. I came from Fano, but I died away from home, in a region where I thought I would be safe. Azzo of Este had me killed. I was taken by surprise, and if I had fled toward Mira I would still be alive. Instead, I fled into a swamp and the reeds slowed me down and tripped me and I was slaughtered and watched the blood flow out of my body and form a pool."

Dante thought, *I have heard of this person. This is Jacopo del Cassero, who opposed Azzo VIII, who was both powerful and without pity. In 1298, Jacopo was traveling to Milan, but Azzo sent assassins to ambush him at the town of Oriago. As Jacopo said, he died a violent death.*

A second soul said, "I hope that your journey up the mountain will be successful, and I hope that you will help me. I am Buonconte, and I am from Montefeltro. No one — not even my wife, Giovanna, cares for me. I am ashamed."

Dante thought, *Apparently, no one — not even his wife, Giovanna — is saying prayers for his soul.*

Dante asked, "No one ever found the place where you were buried. What happened to your body?"

Buonconte of Montefeltro replied, "In 1289 I led my forces — the Ghibellines of Arezzo — against the Guelfs of Florence. In this battle — the Battle of Campaldino — I was defeated and mortally wounded. I made my way to the river Archiano. My throat was an open wound. I went blind from loss of blood. I murmured one word — 'Mary' — and I shed a tear of true repentance. Then I died.

"Because I had repented at the very last moment of life, an angel from Paradise and a fiend from the Inferno showed up. The angel took my soul, and the fiend said, 'You are stealing what I thought would be mine. But although you have charge of Buonconte's immortal soul because of a single word and a single tear, I am taking charge of what remains of his mortal part: his corpse.' The fiend called up a storm, great torrents of water fell from the stormy sky, and my corpse was swept into the river Arno."

Dante thought, *The father of Buonconte of Montefeltro is Guido da Montefeltro, whom I saw in the Inferno. Their stories are very different. Guido da Montefeltro thought that he was going to Paradise, and Saint Francis even came for his soul, but a black devil intervened and pointed out that Guido had not truly repented his sins. So at the last moment, his soul was snatched into Hell. Buonconte of Montefeltro, however, called on Mary's name at the last moment of his life, and at the last moment he truly repented his sins and therefore he will eventually be in Paradise. Guido attempted to scam God with a fake repentance. Pope Boniface VIII scammed Guido into going back to his evil ways. In contrast, Buonconte's repentance is sincere. He utters one sincere word with his last breath, and that is enough to save him. The devil that comes to collect Buonconte's soul is angry and abuses his corpse, but the corpse is not important — the soul is. Repentance must be sincere; no one gets away with trying to scam God. It is interesting to note that my political enemies can make it into Paradise. I was a Guelf, and Buonconte was a Ghibelline, an enemy of the Guelfs, but Buonconte will make it into Paradise.*

Then a third soul, a woman, spoke to Dante: "After you have rested from your journey once you are back in the Land of the Living, please remember me. My name is Pia. I was born in Siena; I died in Maremna. My husband, who pledged faith to me when he put a ring on my finger, killed me."

Dante thought, *This is La Pia, whose jealous husband thought that she had committed adultery and threw her out of a window. I spoke to only one woman — Francesca da Rimini — in the Inferno. La Pia is the first woman I have spoken to on the Mountain of Purgatory. The two souls are very different. La Pia is courteous. She wants me to remember her after I am rested from his journey. La Pia is simply charming. La Pia also sincerely repented her sins. Francesca put herself at the center of the universe, while La Pia wants me to rest first, and then remember her. These souls in Prepurgatory want me to remember them. One reason, of course, is that souls in Purgatory will benefit from prayers that are said for them. Living people do pray for the souls of deceased loved ones, and if we are pure of heart, our prayers will be heard in Heaven. The souls in Prepurgatory also want loved ones to know that they — the souls in Prepurgatory — will make it to Paradise.*

Chapter 6: Prepurgatory — Sordello (Purgatory)

Think of the ending of a game of dice. The loser stays behind, replaying each throw of the dice in his mind, suddenly aware that he should not have played the game.

The winner walks away with many newfound friends, all congratulating him on his good fortune and all hoping for a portion of that good fortune. Most of the newfound friends block his exit except for the fortunate few to whom he gives a coin. To the others he gives promises and eventually is able to depart.

So Dante was surrounded by souls requesting to be remembered in the Land of the Living so that they would be prayed for and be able to more quickly climb the Mountain of Purgatory, the task that God had set for them.

As Dante was surrounded, souls spoke to him and told him who they are. Although he had not recognized these souls, they were well known enough that he had heard of them.

Dante saw Benincasa of Laterina here. As a judge in the city of Arezzo, Benincasa gave the brother of the notorious bandit Ghino di Tacco the death sentence. Beincasa became a judge in Rome, and to get revenge for his brother's death, Ghino disguised himself and burst into Benincasa's courtroom in Rome, cut off Benincasa's head, and escaped with it.

Dante also saw here Pierre de la Brosse of Turenne, who was accused by Mary of Brabant, the second wife of Philip III of France, of having corresponded with King Alfonso X of Castile, Philip's enemy, with whom he was warring. Mary caused forged correspondence to be created, and in 1278, Pierre was hanged, thus dying of violence like the other saved souls in this group.

Eventually, Dante and Virgil were able to free themselves from this group of souls and continue climbing upward.

Dante, however, was puzzled. He said to Virgil, "I have read, I believe, in your *Aeneid*, that prayers cannot bend the will of Heaven. Aeneas, who came from defeated Troy to Italy to become an important ancestor of the Roman people, went with the Sybil, a prophetess, to the Underworld. On the shore across from the Underworld they saw Palinurus, the pilot of Aeneas' ship, who had drowned. Palinurus' body had not been found and buried, and until it had a funeral, or a hundred years had passed, Chiron the ferryman would not allow him to cross the river and reach the Underworld. Palinurus hoped that Aeneas would pray to his mother, the goddess Venus, for permission to take him across with them to the Underworld. The Sybil who guides Aeneas through the Underworld replied to Palinurus, 'What hopes delude you, wretched soul? Do you think that, thus unburied, you will cross the river and view the Furies and infernal gods, and visit, without burial, the dark abodes? You must wait for your proper time to enter the Underworld. Fate, and the dooming gods, are deaf to prayer.'

"Is it possible that I am misunderstanding the meaning of this passage?"

Virgil replied, "What I wrote there is true, but it does not mean that these souls on the Mountain of Purgatory are wrong when they tell you that prayers will hasten their progress up the Mountain of Purgatory.

"Love can wipe clean the debts that these saved souls owe. The prayers of the pure are heard in Paradise.

"The passage from my *Aeneid* that you quoted refers to a different kind of prayer, a kind of prayer that is not heard in Paradise. The prayers of those who will be damned are not heard in Paradise.

"But soon another will make the meaning of what I say clearer. You know that other: Beatrice, whom you loved and love. You will see her at the top of this mountain. You will see that she is blessed and smiling."

Dante said, "Let's pick up the pace. I am eager to see Beatrice. Before, I was tired, but now I am refreshed and eager to travel quickly. Time is passing. It is afternoon now, as I can see by the shadow of this mountain. I am not casting a shadow now. I am in shade."

Virgil replied, "As long as we have daylight, we will climb, but climbing will take time, and we will not do it in one day. But look, a solitary saved soul is ahead. We can ask him what is the best place to climb upward."

Dante and Virgil approached the soul, who quietly and warily watched them.

Virgil spoke to him and asked which was the best place to climb upward, but the soul ignored the question and instead asked from which city they had come in the Land of the Living.

Virgil began his answer, "Mantua ...."

The soul did not wait for the rest of the answer. He jumped up and said, "My name is Sordello, and I am from the same city," and he embraced Virgil.

Dante the Pilgrim reflected, *This kind of friendly, happy embrace did not happen in the Inferno. I saw no loving hugs in the Inferno. This soul is happy to meet a person who is from his city. He regards its citizens as his friends. Such was not the case when I met Farinata in the Inferno. Farinata, who is from my own city, Florence, regarded me only as a person who could give him information and as a person whom he could triumph over by telling me bad news. Farinata revels in destructive factionalism, and I fell into the trap of dueling verbally with him. Farinata pointed out that he had scattered my party twice, and I pointed out that my party had returned to Florence but that Farinata's family had not. Our arguing with each other was easy to do, since he is a Ghibelline and I am a Guelf. Unless I can refrain from the destructive factionalism that destroys cities and countries, I can end up in the Inferno like Farinata.*

Dante the Poet was seized with a cold fury: *Italy, you are the land of bad factionalism. You are divided, not united, and you lack a good political leader. This soul and Virgil know no factionalism but instead rejoice in being citizens of the same city. But in Italy, civil war reigns even inside one city, as well as city against city and region against region. Is any part of Italy truly at peace?*

Justinian repaired the Roman law, which is one of the wonders of the world, but that does no good because no one is around to enforce it. Why isn't the Holy Roman Emperor — Albert I of Hapsburg, Germany — around? In part, because Pope Boniface VIII doesn't want him around. In a much better world, a good Holy Roman Emperor would enforce the secular law and a good Pope would handle religious matters. The two would work together instead of opposing each other. But Albert I of Hapsburg ignores Italy, which has factionalism between such families as the Capulets and the Montagues. Instead of coming to Italy, the Holy Roman Emperor stays north, and peace is there but not in Italy.

Law is enormously important in society. It lets people know what they can and cannot do legally. If the laws were not written down, people would find it difficult to know when they were breaking the law. Florence and other places are chaotic because of constantly changing laws. When the Ghibellines kick out the Guelfs, they make new laws. When the Guelfs kick out the Ghibellines, they make new laws. With political power changing hands so quickly and so often, it is very difficult to make plans. In order for people to respect law, it has to stay law for a while. If it changes frequently, people won't know what is legal and what is illegal.

Italy lacks good leaders. It has fools who call themselves leaders.

Florence, my own city, you should be but are not exempt from my criticism. Other cities have citizens who think about what needs to be done and how to go about doing it. First they think, and then they do. But the citizens of Florence speak first and never think. They say, but they never do. Other cities have citizens who think twice before running for political office in order to make sure that they are worthy of serving the public and can do the job well. But the citizens of Florence eagerly run for political office without being competent enough to serve the public. And Florence, you are a model of inconsistency. With the bad factionalism in Florence, one political group seizes power, and then a different political group seizes power. Laws passed in October are overturned in November. Citizens who would like to obey the laws cannot because the laws change so frequently. And a citizen who does an action that is legal in October can be accused of breaking the law later because the legal action that they performed in October is illegal in November. They can be accused of breaking the law even when they don't do that action in November and did it only in October. And not only the laws and politicians change. So do the currency and customs.

Though your citizens should lie in luxury, it is as if they are lying in a hospital bed.

Chapter 7: Prepurgatory — The Negligent Princes (Purgatory)

Sordello and Virgil embraced three or four times.

Dante thought, *I have heard of Sordello. He was a poet of both political and moral poetry, and he was a climber into the bedroom windows of many women. He was passionate about politics as well and denounced political corruption.*

Then Sordello asked, "Who are you? What are your names?"

Virgil replied, "Before the Harrowing of Hell, in which many souls were taken to this mountain, the Roman Emperor Caesar Augustus, previously known as Octavian, buried me. I am Virgil. I lost residence in Paradise not for any fault in virtue, but because I lacked Christian faith."

Sordello was both believing and disbelieving. "This cannot be the truth — but it is the truth!" Sordello again embraced Virgil, but this time he knelt and embraced Virgil's knees to show respect to him.

Sordello said to Virgil, "You are the glory of the Romans. You showed that the greatest poetry could be written in Latin. You are the greatest of poets. How am I worthy — or lucky — enough to see you? Are you from the Inferno, and if you are, from what part?"

Dante thought, *Sordello has his faults, although he is a saved soul. He was alone when we met him, but this mountain is a place of community. He was happy to learn that Virgil, whose identity he did not then know, is from his own city, but he ought to be friends with people from other places as well. One day, he will be a citizen of Paradise, whose inhabitants come from many cities.*

Also, Virgil asked him for directions, but Sordello ignored that request, although this is a place where one can ask for help and usually get it. Sordello apparently was hoping to find someone from his own hometown, which is a form of community. Sordello is a hero-worshipper — as am I. When he learned Virgil's identity, he was so star-struck that he stopped listening to Virgil's explanation of where he came from — Limbo — and why he is there. We both adore the poetry of Virgil. But Sordello so hero-worships Virgil that he is ignoring me, who is standing next to him. Also, Sordello is so impressed by Virgil that he is forgetting to keep his eyes on the prize. Still, Sordello is a saved soul. One need not be perfect — which

Virgil replied to Sordello, "Through all the circles of the Inferno, I have come to this mountain. I am here on a mission from a Heavenly lady. I am denied entrance into Paradise not because of any sin I committed but because of a lack of Christian faith. In the Inferno is a place where sighs are heard instead of shrieks. The sadness of the souls there is due to being separated from God. I am there with unbaptized children who still have the sin of Adam. I am there with those who had the four cardinal virtues of Prudence, Temperance, Justice, and Fortitude in abundance, but lacked the three theological virtues of Faith, Hope, and Charity.

"But can you help us? We need to climb higher and find the path to where Purgatory Proper begins. Can you help us find that path?"

Sordello replied, "Souls in Prepurgatory can go where they wish in Prepurgatory, and so I will be your guide as far as I am allowed to climb. But now night is coming, and it is forbidden to climb higher during the night, so let us find a good place to sleep. To the right is a group of souls that I think you would like to see. With your permission, I will take you there."

Virgil asked, "Why can't a soul climb higher during the night? Would someone or something stop him physically? Or would the will of the soul be such that the soul cannot climb higher?"

Sordello used a finger to draw a line on the ground of the upward slope and said, "After nightfall, you would not be able to move past this line. The shadows of night sap the soul and make it unable to move higher. During the night, we can move down the slope, but not up the slope."

Virgil, surprised by what he had heard, said, "Then please take us to the place you mentioned so that we can rest."

They walked and they came to a valley and looked down into it.

Sordello said, "Now we will go a little further and then rest."

The valley was beautiful both in color and in scent. The sound coming from the residents of the valley was also beautiful. It was the song *Salve Regina*, or "Hail, Holy Queen," a song to Mary, mother of Jesus:

"Hail, holy Queen, Mother of Mercy!

"Our life, our sweetness, and our hope!

"To you do we cry, poor banished children of Eve,

"To you do we send up our sighs,

"Mourning and weeping in this valley of tears.

"Turn, then, most gracious advocate,

"Your eyes of mercy toward us;

"And after this our exile show unto us the

"Blessed fruit of your womb — Jesus —

"O clement, O loving, O sweet virgin Mary."

Dante looked down into the valley, and there he saw saved souls.

Sordello said, "Please don't ask me to take you down into the valley until after the Sun has set. From here, you can easily see the faces of the saved souls."

Sordello then explained the identities of these saved souls:

"Rudolf of Hapsburg concerned himself with political affairs in Germany and ignored those of Italy. If only he had thought about Italy, he could have united it. Because he ignored Italy, he now looks as if he has left something undone that should have been done. The other rulers are singing, but he is not. Rudolf of Hapsburg was a Negligent Ruler.

"Ottokar II, King of Bohemia, was Rudolf's enemy, but now he comforts him. While alive, Ottokar II twice rebelled against Rudolf, failing both times. The second time, this valiant warrior died in battle. Ottokar II is a good father who had a bad son: Wenceslaus. Ottokar II was a Negligent Ruler.

"Philip III of France, who has a snub nose, fathered Philip IV, who is also known as Philip the Fair. Philip III is a good father who had a bad son. Philip III was a Negligent Ruler.

"Henry the Fat of Novarre, who looks kind, died by being suffocated with his own fat. Henry the Fat's daughter married Philip the Fair, aka the Plague of France. Henry the Fat was a Negligent Ruler.

"Peter III of Aragon, who looks sturdy, married Constance, the daughter of Manfred. Peter III was a Negligent Ruler.

"Charles I of Anjou, who has a big nose, defeated Manfred at Benevento in 1266. In life, Peter III and Charles I were enemies, but now they are reconciled. Charles I's son, Charles II, was not as good as his father. Charles I was a Negligent Ruler.

"Alfonso III of Aragon is the eldest son of Peter III of Aragon. In this case, a good father had a good son. However, Peter III's other two sons — James II of

Aragon and Frederick II of Sicily — were bad sons. Alfonso III was a Negligent Ruler.

"All too often, a good father has a bad son. Nobility of character is not acquired by birth.

"Henry III of England was strong in faith, but he attended so many masses that he ignored his duties as King of England. Henry III was a Negligent Ruler.

"William VII, also known as Longsword, was the Marquis of Montferrat. He failed to stop a revolt in the city of Alessandria, was taken prisoner, and was kept in an iron cage and displayed to the public until he died. William VII was a Negligent Ruler."

Dante thought, *Most of the Negligent Rulers were negligent in taking care of their own souls. They kept God waiting, so God is keeping them waiting for a while before he allows them into Purgatory Proper. They were so occupied with Earthly matters that they had no time for Heavenly matters. In addition, they sometimes didn't do very well in taking care of Earthly matters. One ruler — Henry III of England — was noted for his piety. His negligence was toward his kingdom. Kings must take care of their spiritual as well as of their secular matters. A good King can do much good for his people, but of course, a good King must also take care of his own soul. God wants Kings to be good to the people they rule.*

We also see that bad sons can be born to good fathers, and no doubt good sons can be born to bad fathers. Nobility of character is an acquired, not hereditary, virtue.

We also see that no one has to be perfect — an impossibility for mortal men and women — to climb the Mountain of Purgatory and enter Paradise.

We also see that enemies are reconciled in Prepurgatory. In the Inferno, enemies were not reconciled.

During my day in Prepurgatory, I have seen many saved souls. The souls of dead sinners who sincerely repented their sins arrive in Prepurgatory, where they wait until they are ready to pass through the Gate of Purgatory to Purgatory Proper. A number of groups of people have to wait to climb the Mountain of Purgatory, but waiting is proper for them. These souls — the late repentant — must wait longer than others. The late repentant are these:

1) those who died while excommunicated.

2) the slothful (who kept putting off spiritual matters).

3) those who repented only in their final — sometimes violent — moments of life.

4) those who ignored spiritual matters while concentrating on worldly matters, and those who ignored worldly matters while concentrating on spiritual matters (the Negligent Rulers).

These souls kept God waiting, and God makes them wait to enter Purgatory Proper. However, I have learned that these souls can enter Purgatory Proper more quickly if good people pray for them.

Chapter 8: Prepurgatory — The Serpent and the Two Angels (Purgatory)

Now was the hour when sailors, on their first day's journey away from home, think of home and loved ones. Now was the hour when a traveler hears the tolling of a far-away bell and thinks of loved ones.

Dante looked at a soul who rose and began singing "*Te Lucis Ante Terminum*" — "Before the End of the Light." The saved soul looked to the East and seemed to be thinking only of God.

The soul sang beautifully, and the other souls joined in the singing as they looked at the stars and sang a prayer asking to be kept safe that night:

"You, before the close of day

"Creator of the world, we pray

"That with Your wonted favor,

"You would be our Guard and Keeper now.

"From all ill dreams defend our eyes,

"From nightly fears and fantasies:

"Tread under foot our ghostly foe,

"That no pollution we may know.

"O Father, may what we ask be done

"Through Jesus Christ Your only Son,

"Who, with the Holy Ghost and You,

"Shall live and reign eternally.

"Amen."

Dante the Poet thought, *Reader, sharpen your eyes and learn. This prayer has been and will be answered.*

Dante the Pilgrim saw descending from Paradise two angels who each carried a blunt sword. The angels' clothing was green, as were their wings. One angel landed on a bank above, and the other angel landed on the bank opposite. Dante could easily see the angels' gold hair, but their faces were so bright that he could not see them.

Sordello said, "Mary has sent the two angels to protect us from the serpent in the valley. The serpent will soon arrive."

Dante was afraid. He did not know from which direction the serpent would come, and he moved closer to his protector, Virgil.

Then Sordello said, "You have seen the angels. We can now descend into the valley."

Sordello thought, *It is important that you see the angels. They show that God is our protector.*

To descend into the valley took only three steps. Dante saw a soul looking at him, attempting to see his face in the fast-arriving darkness.

The soul moved toward Dante, and they recognized each other, rejoiced, and greeted each other.

Dante thought, *This is my friend Nino Visconti, who died in 1296. Although he was active in worldly affairs, he did not let them corrupt his soul.*

After they had greeted each other, Nino said to Dante, "How long has it been since you arrived here in the angel's boat?"

Dante replied, "I came here by a different journey. I traveled through the Inferno. I am still alive, but I hope that by taking this journey, I will come to this mountain after I die."

Nino was amazed. So was Sordello, who had ignored Dante since learning Virgil's identity. Because Dante had been in the shadow of the mountain, he had not cast a shadow, and so Sordello had not realized that Dante was still living.

Both Sordello and Nino backed away from Dante, and then Sordello turned to face Virgil as Nino called to a nearby soul, "Corrado, come here! See something marvelous that God has willed!"

Nino said to Dante, "Since you are still living, I beg you to do me a favor. When you are back in the Land of the Living, please tell my daughter, Giovanna, to pray for me so that I may climb this mountain sooner. Her mother has forgotten me. She has remarried. Her new husband is a man who will bring her less honor than marriage to me did."

Nino's face was indignant as he thought of his widow's new marriage.

Dante looked at the sky, and he saw three new stars that had superseded the four stars that he had seen when he first reached the mountain.

Virgil asked, "What are you looking at?"

Dante replied, "At the three bright stars that light up the sky above the South Pole."

Virgil said, "With the passage of time, and the movement of the cosmos, the four stars you saw earlier have moved out of your sight. These have taken their place."

Dante the Poet thought, *The four stars I saw earlier represent the four cardinal virtues: Prudence, Temperance, Justice, and Fortitude. These three stars represent the three theological virtues: Faith, Hope, and Charity.*

Sordello grabbed Virgil's arm and said, "The serpent is coming."

The serpent came leisurely through the valley, even stopping to lick its back as if proudly grooming itself.

The angels flew down toward the serpent, and the serpent took flight. The angels flew back to their posts.

Dante the Poet thought, *God could — of course — destroy the serpent, but He does not. He allows this ritual to be repeated each evening. This ritual bears a message: I will protect you, and I will answer your prayers. The saved souls know that they are in no danger from the serpent — the angels are bearing blunted swords because sharp swords are not needed here. However, the saved souls watch this ritual because God is showing them that He keeps His promises and that He answers prayers. Of course, all these souls want to climb the mountain, and God is letting them know that yes, eventually they can climb the mountain. Also, of course, God is a Protector in addition to a Promise-Keeper.*

Nino had called Corrado over to see Dante.

Dante the Poet thought, *This is Corrado Malaspina. When I am in exile, I will shelter for a while with the Malaspina family, which is known throughout Europe for its generosity.*

Corrado said to Dante the Pilgrim, "I wish you well in your journey up the mountain. If you can tell me recent news of the Magra Valley, please do so. I came from there, and I was well known there. My name is Corrado Malaspina — the younger one."

Dante replied to Corrado, "I have never visited that region, but all of Europe knows your family, which is famous for its hospitality and its generosity. While other families have failed in virtue, your family has not."

Corrado replied, "Within seven years, you will know much better the hospitality and generosity of my family."

Dante the Poet thought, *This is a prophecy that did come true.*

Chapter 9: Prepurgatory — First Prophetic Dream and Saint Peter's Gate (Purgatory)

In Italy, dawn was arriving and the Sun appearing. On the mountain, night and the Moon had arrived. In the hour before dawn, sometimes dreams are true.

Dante fell asleep, and he dreamed that an eagle with golden feathers was soaring in the sky and was ready to swoop down, just as Jupiter, disguised as an eagle, had swooped down and seized the young Ganymede, the most beautiful mortal alive, to serve as cupbearer to the gods on Mount Olympus.

In his dream, Dante watched the eagle circling in the air, and then the eagle swooped down and seized him, just as the disguised Jupiter had seized Ganymede. The eagle soared with Dante to the sphere of fire, and then both Dante and the eagle seemed to burn, and Dante woke up.

In Paradise, an angel thought, *The medieval conception of the cosmos was that the Earth is at the center of the universe. People believed that over the Earth are a number of crystalline spheres, one of which is a sphere of fire. That is the sphere that Dante the Pilgrim is dreaming of here. The medieval conception of the cosmos was that other spheres held the Sun, the Moon, various planets, and the fixed stars (they are fixed in placement to each other; in contrast, the planets are not fixed in placement to each other). The modern conception of the cosmos is much different; modern scientists think of the cosmos as consisting mostly of empty space and dark matter and dark energy. Medieval thinkers believed that each celestial sphere made contact with the sphere above it and with the sphere below it.*

When Dante woke up, he did not know where he was. When he had fallen asleep, he had been with Virgil, Sordello, Nino Visconti, and Corrado Malaspina. Now he was in a new place. He reflected that he was as confused as the young Achilles must have been when his mother, the goddess Thetis, had taken him while he was asleep away from his tutor, the Centaur Chiron, in Thessaly, to the island Skyros to live, disguised as a young woman, among the women in the palace of King Lycomedes. Thetis' plan failed to keep Achilles out of the Trojan War. Ulysses and Diomed came to the palace and showed jewelry and weapons to the women (and the disguised Achilles) of the palace. The women were interested in the jewelry, Achilles was interested in the weapons, and Ulysses and Diomed carried Achilles off to fight and die in the Trojan War.

Dante was dazed and confused by his surroundings, but Virgil explained what had happened and where he was.

Virgil said, "Do not be afraid. We have made much progress on our journey. Let us keep going. You are now before the gate leading to Purgatory. Look at the cleft in that rock there. That is where the gate to Purgatory is located.

"Before dawn arrived, a lady from Paradise — Saint Lucia — came to us. She said to me, 'I am Lucia. Let me take this sleeping man and speed him on his way.' Sordello and the other saved souls remained behind; they are not ready to climb this high.

"Saint Lucia carried you in her arms here. I followed. With her beautiful eyes, she let me know where the gate to Purgatory is located, and then she left, and you woke up."

Dante felt relieved. He thought, *I am becoming aware of reality and learning truth. Before, I was thinking of Jupiter kidnapping a young boy. Then I thought of something better: a mother trying, but unfortunately failing, to protect her son. Then I learned the reality and the truth, which are best: A Heavenly lady is seeking to save the soul of a sinner and providing impressive aid to make that happen.*

Dante also thought, *While living, Saint Lucia was persecuted and tortured — including being blinded — because she was a Christian. In Paradise, her eyes have been restored to her.*

Dante was ready to climb higher. He and Virgil approached the gate leading to Purgatory. Leading to the gate were three steps; each step was a different color.

Sitting on the highest step was an angel. Dante lifted his eyes to look at the angel, but the angel's face was too bright to look at, so Dante looked down again.

The angel carried an unsheathed sword. It also was too bright to look at.

The angel said to Dante and Virgil, "Stay where you are and answer me. Why are you here, and where is your guide? You must have permission to pass through the gate."

Virgil replied, "A lady from Paradise has given us permission to pass through the gate. She said to me on behalf of this man, 'Behold the gate. Go through it and continue your journey up the mountain.'"

The angel courteously said, "May the lady from Paradise continue to help you. Come forward and climb the stairs."

The first step was white, the second step was darker than purple-black, and the third step was red.

Dante thought, *The three colors represent the three stages of repentance:*

1) self-examination: white,

2) sorrow for sin, contrition: darker than purple-black, and

3) penance: red.

The angel rested his feet upon the third step, and he sat on a sill (a slab of stone at the bottom of a gateway) that seemed to be made of adamantine rock. Adamantine is a legendarily hard mineral that cannot be broken.

The three steps and the one sill combined make up the number four, which suggests the four stages of human freedom:

1) innocence (white). We are born innocent.

2) fall (black). All of us sin.

3) redemption (red). Jesus has redeemed us by bleeding and dying on the cross.

4) freedom from sin (an adamantine will that rejects sin and cannot be broken). In Paradise, our souls will be perfected, and we will no longer sin.

Of course, the souls climbing the Mountain of Purgatory are working to purge their sins and perfect their souls so that they can enter Paradise. Their souls are seeking to move from *posse non peccare* to *non posse peccare*.

Human beings have free will, and this means that they can choose to sin or to not sin.

If a human being chooses to sin, their will is *posse peccare*: able to sin. A person who sins habitually can become a slave to sin and can lose their free will. Consider addiction to tobacco. If we are supposed to keep our bodies healthy, then smoking tobacco is a sin. People who become addicted to tobacco can lose their free will. They may grow to hate the habit and greatly desire to quit, but they find that they cannot. They no longer have the ability to quit, for they have lost their free will.

If a human being chooses to not sin, their will is *posse non peccare*: able to not sin. The person could have sinned but chose not to.

A person who chooses over and over to do something can develop their free will so that the person can easily do what the person wants to do. Consider exercise. A person who chooses to exercise before or after work each day and does so consistently will soon find it easy to begin exercising at the proper time and place they have chosen. It can become difficult to skip a day of exercise.

A person who chooses over and over not to sin can develop their free will so that the person can easily do what the person wants to do. A person can become so accustomed to not sinning that it can be difficult to sin. A person can develop such a hatred of sin that it becomes impossible to sin. On the Mountain of Purgatory, souls are developing the ability to *non posse peccare*: to not be able to sin.

Such souls still have free will because they can do what they want to do. A smoker who wants to quit but cannot has lost his or her free will. The souls on the Mountain of Purgatory are working to purge their souls and to avoid sin. They want to not sin, and they are developing their free will so that they will always choose not to sin. They are doing what they want to do: They want to do the right thing, and they in fact do the right thing. They choose not to sin — every time.

Dante and Virgil climbed the steps, and Virgil said to Dante, "Ask the angel now, humbly, to turn the keys and let us through the gate."

Dante knelt and begged the angel to let him and his companion through the gate.

First, the angel carved with his sword seven P's on Dante's forehead and told Dante, "Make sure that you heal these seven wounds as you journey up the mountain."

The angel thought, The P is an abbreviation for Peccatum, *the Latin word for "sin." All who journey up the mountain will heal seven wounds. Pride is the foundation of all sins; pride makes a person think that he or she is the center of the universe. These are the seven wounds, and these are illustrations of how these sinners think:*

1) Pride — A sinner who is guilty of Pride thinks, "I am the center of the universe, and I am better than other people. Quite simply, I am more important than other people."

2) Envy — A sinner who is guilty of Envy thinks, "I am the center of the universe, and if you have something I want, I envy you."

3) Wrath — A sinner who is guilty of Wrath thinks, "Because I am the center of the universe, everything ought to go my way, and when it does not, I get angry."

4) Sloth — A sinner who is guilty of Sloth thinks, "I am the center of the universe, so I don't have to work at something. Either other people can do my work for me, or they can give me credit for work I have not done because if I had done the work, I would have done it excellently."

5) Avariciousness and Prodigality — A sinner who is guilty of Avariciousness or Prodigality thinks, "I am the center of the universe, so I deserve to have what I want. If I want money, I get money and never spend it, or if I want the things that money can buy, then I spend every penny I can make or borrow to get what I want. Either way, I deserve to have what I want."

6) Gluttony — A sinner who is guilty of Gluttony thinks, "I am the center of the universe, so I deserve these three extra pieces of pie every night. This is my reward for myself for being so fabulous."

7) Lust — A sinner who is guilty of Lust thinks, "I am the center of the universe, so my needs take precedence over the needs of everyone else. If I want to get laid, it's OK if I lie to get someone in the sack and never call that person afterward. My sexual pleasure is more important than the hurt of someone who realizes that he or she has been used."

As saved souls climb the mountain, they will purge each of these deadly sins. They will learn some examples of the sins and they will learn some examples of the virtues that are opposed to the sins:

Ledge 1: Sin — Pride; Virtue — Humility

Ledge 2: Sin — Envy; Virtue — Kindness and Love of Others

Ledge 3: Sin — Wrath; Virtue — Meekness and Patience

Ledge 4: Sin — Sloth; Virtue — Zeal and Diligence

Ledge 5: Sin — Avariciousness (and Wastefulness); Virtue — Charity and Detachment from Riches and Detachment from What Riches can Buy

Ledge 6: Sin — Gluttony; Virtue — Abstinence or Temperance

Ledge 7: Sin — Lust; Virtue — Chastity or Proper Sex

The angel wore a robe that was the color of ashes: the color of penitence. From beneath the robe he took out two keys: one was gold and one was silver.

The angel inserted both keys and turned them one at a time.

The angel said, "If either of these keys does not turn, the gate will not open. One key is more precious than the other, but both are precious."

The angel thought, *The gold key is the God-given authority to absolve — forgive — a person who has sinned. The silver key is the act of absolution. To be absolved of sin, a person must really repent sin and not be trying to scam God.*

The angel said, "Peter gave me these keys and told me to err on the side of mercy, saying, 'It is better to admit too many than to admit too few. They must ask for mercy.'"

Dante thought, *Jesus gave keys to Peter in Matthew 16:18-19: "And I say also to you, That you are Peter, and upon this rock I will build my Church; and the gates of hell shall not prevail against it. And I will give to you the keys of the kingdom of Heaven: and whatsoever you shall bind on earth shall be bound in Heaven: and whatsoever you shall loose on earth shall be loosed in Heaven."*

The angel pushed against the gate, and it swung open.

The angel said, "Go through the gate, but don't look back, or you will find yourself in Prepurgatory again."

The gate creaked as it swung open, but Dante heard the souls in Purgatory Proper rejoice as another soul joined them. The rejoicing souls sang the "*Te Deum Laudamus*" — "You, O Lord, We Praise," of which these are the first few lines:

"Lord God, Your praise we sing;

"Lord God, our thanks we bring;

"Father in eternity,

"All the world worships You.

"Angels all and Heavenly host

"Of Your glory loudly boast;

"Both Cherubim and Seraphim

"Sing ever with loud voice this hymn:

"Holy are You, our God!

"Holy are You, our God!

"Holy are You, our God, the Creator and Lord of All!"

The creaking of the gate made it difficult for Dante the Pilgrim to hear some of the words being sung, just as at church a worshipper may not hear some words of a hymn because of the music of the organ.

Dante the Poet thought, *At this time, I was not yet a perfected soul. I was required to spend time in Prepurgatory in part to learn that one can prepare to be a perfected soul before one dies and before one enters Purgatory Proper. One way to do that, of course, is through the sincere repentance of one's sins. Another way is through religious songs. The main point is this: Don't wait before repenting and before beginning the process of purging your sins.*

Chapter 10: First Ledge — Pride (Purgatory)

Dante and Virgil walked through the gate, and they did not look back. The people who walk through that gate learn to love the right things for the right reasons and with the right intensity.

Then they climbed a narrow, zigzagging path through a cleft in the mountain.

Virgil advised Dante, "Walk carefully."

Finally, they walked through the metaphorical eye of the needle and reached the first ledge of Purgatory Proper, which has seven ledges, each devoted to purging a particular sin. This ledge is not wide: It is the width of three men's bodies, lying end to end.

Dante looked at the side of the mountain, which was sheer and impossible to climb. The mountain's side was pure white marble, a sculptor's dream, and an Artist who was better than the ancient Greek sculptor Polycletus, the greatest of all human sculptors, carved it. The Artist who had carved the mountain was also a better Artist than nature.

Dante thought, *God is the sculptor here; God created the art on the Mountain of Purgatory. Previously I learned that He is an architect — when He built the Gate to the Inferno. Now I see that He is a great sculptor, too.*

Dante looked and saw an exemplum of humility or lack of pride: Mary and the Annunciation. He thought, *When the angel announces to Mary that she will give birth to the Messiah, Mary could have understandably been proud. Instead, she gave all glory to God and called herself a servant (handmaid) of God.*

The carving was so well done that speech seemed visible. As Dante looked at the carving, he seemed to hear the angel say, "*Ave,*" as in "Hail, Mary." And he seemed to hear Mary reply to the angel, "*Ecce ancilla Dei,*" or "Behold the handmaid of God."

Virgil watched Dante look at this carving for a while and then suggested, "Why don't you look at the other carvings as well?"

Dante looked ahead and saw another carving and moved closer to it. Here in the marble he saw oxen and a cart bearing the Ark of the Covenant: a chest containing the stone tablets on which the Ten Commandments were written. In the carving, King David showed humility by dancing as the ark is brought into Jerusalem. In contrast to the humility of David, his first wife, Michal, shows scorn for her husband, as he dances with his robes pulled up, revealing his legs. Because Michal was so proud, God punished her by making her barren: She could not bear children. In the sculpture, incense came from censers, and Dante seemed to smell the incense as he looked at the carving. Dante also seemed to hear the singing of the choirs as the ark entered Jerusalem.

Beatrice looked down from Paradise and thought, *All of these carvings are important, but Dante, pay special attention to this carving. King David is especially noted for these things: 1) He is a great politician: a King. 2) He is a great poet: the author of the Psalms. 3) He is a great sinner who was saved by God. 4) He is a very talented man, just like Ulysses and Guido da Montefeltro in the Inferno. Fortunately, David repented. And he had a lot to repent. From a rooftop, David once saw a woman bathing, and he desired her. Because he was King, he was able to sleep with her, although she was married — her husband (Uriah the Hittite) was away on a military mission. Because of King David, she got pregnant. David sent for her husband so that he (her husband) would have sex with Bathsheba and so think the child was his, but her husband did not want to have sex while people were dying in war. (David should have been fighting, not committing adultery.) Therefore, King David ordered that Bathsheba's husband be put in the front lines where he would probably be killed, and he was killed. Other people were killed with Uriah. Bad battle tactics were needed to get Uriah killed, and other innocent men died with him. David then made Bathsheba one of his wives. This story does have a happy ending, as David repents his sin, is forgiven, and is now in Paradise. You, Dante, are very much like David in being a great poet and a mostly successful politician. Of course, both you and David are highly intelligent people. Dante, you have also sinned, and you can learn a lot from David. You need to learn to be humble: to give credit to God and not to yourself. You also need to learn to repent your sins.*

Dante then moved to see a third carving, one that showed the humility of the Roman Emperor Trajan. On his way to fight a war, Emperor Trajan spoke to a poor widow who wanted him to give her justice for her son who had been killed. At first, Emperor Trajan wanted her to wait for justice in the murder of her son until he came back from a military campaign, but she asked him, "What if you don't come back?" Emperor Trajan said, "Then whoever replaces me will give you justice." The widow replied, "How can you let another person's virtue do what you should do?" He then agreed to give justice to her for her son's death, saying, "Justice demands that I perform my duty." All of this conversation Dante seemed to hear as he looked at the carving. God is such a good sculptor that He can create visible speech.

By looking at the carvings, Dante understood that good art can lead to education. For example, to understand something, look at examples of it. He would soon learn that one should look also at examples of its opposite. For example, to understand humility, look at examples of humility and at examples of pride.

Dante thought, *We need to tell the right kinds of stories, and we need good role models, and we need the ability to identify bad role models.*

Virgil said to Dante, "Look at the crowd of souls slowly approaching us. They will be able to tell us how to climb further up the mountain."

Dante the Pilgrim now looked and saw something, but what exactly it was he could not make out. He said to Virgil, "Some things seem to be moving toward us, but they do not appear to be souls. What are they? I can't make them out."

Virgil explained, "These souls are being purged of pride. Because they were proud, each now humbly bends toward the ground. Look closely. You can see huge stones, and underneath each stone is a soul purging its pride. Each soul beats his or her breast."

Dante the Pilgrim thought, *These souls carrying huge stones look like corbels, little sculptures of people that appear in architecture. They sometimes appear to be holding up a roof or other heavy weight such as a column. The souls on the first level of Purgatory Proper look like corbels, and each soul seems to be saying, "I can't go on."*

Dante the Pilgrim noticed that the stones the souls carry are not of equal weight. The prouder a sinner was, the heavier the stone is.

Dante the Poet thought, *Someone may want to say that the repentant sinners are being punished for their sins, but it would be better to say that they are being purged of their sins. The stones the souls are carrying are huge; however, they will gain from all of their hard effort. They will be purged of their sin.*

Although some souls suffer in Purgatory, the purpose of the suffering is to educate the souls and to purge the souls of sin. The souls benefit from their suffering, and they expect to benefit from their suffering. The souls want to be in Purgatory.

They are confident that God will keep His promises and they will reach Paradise. People should keep in mind the purpose of the suffering that takes place in Purgatory.

Christians should also understand that each of us is born to die. When we die, the immortal part goes to God to be judged and leaves the mortal part behind. A living person is defective. Only after purgation of one's sins can a soul be perfected.

A good Christian will avoid pride and so make the perfecting of his or her soul easier.

Chapter 11: First Ledge — Aldobrandesco, Oderisi, Provenzan (Purgatory)

As the souls, burdened with heavy stones, slowly walked on the ledge, they prayed a version of the Lord's Prayer that emphasizes humility:

"Our Father who is in Paradise, by choice, because You love the angels, whom You created before You created Humankind,

"May Humankind, your creation, regard Your name and Your power as holy to show our thanks to You.

"May Your kingdom come and bring us peace, for we cannot attain Your kingdom through our own efforts, but only as Your gift.

"As the angels obey Your will and sing 'Hosannah,' so may Humankind obey Your will.

"Give us this day our daily manna, as You gave manna to others who were in exile from the Holy Land. Without Your blessing, even those who are most eager to go forward will instead go backward.

"And forgive us our sins, as we forgive those who sin against us, although we do not deserve Your forgiveness.

"Although we want to be strong, we recognize that we are weak, and we pray for all Humankind that You lead them not into temptation and instead save them from the Evil One.

"This last request, God, we make not for ourselves, who are saved souls, but for those members of Humankind who are still alive on Earth."

Dante the Poet thought, *The prayers of these souls do good for the living, and the prayers of the living can do much good for the saved souls on the Mountain of Purgatory. Our prayers can help these souls wash away sins and ascend into Paradise more quickly.*

These saved souls, who prayed both for themselves and for others, moved slowly toward Dante and Virgil. Some souls were burdened by heavier stones than other souls — they had been prouder, perhaps of family, talent, or power. They moved as slowly as a man moves in a nightmare when pursued by something or someone who induces panic.

Virgil said to the saved souls, "May justice tempered by mercy free you from the stones and the sins you carry so you may climb up the mountain and reach

Paradise. Please do a good deed now. Please help us. Show us the path by which we may climb to the next ledge of the mountain. This man I am traveling with carries his own burden: the weight of his still-living flesh. Because of that, his progress up the mountain is slow."

Someone answered, but because the souls were bent over by the weight they were carrying, Dante could not see their faces and so did not know which soul had spoken.

However, a soul said, "Walk along the ledge with us, and you will find a place up which you can climb the mountain. If I were not carrying so heavy a weight, I would look up and see if I recognize this still-living man. Perhaps I could move him to feel compassion for me.

"I was an Italian, and my father was a great Tuscan named Guglielmo Aldobrandeschi ... but perhaps you have never heard of him."

Dante thought, *Everyone in Italy knows the name Guglielmo Aldobrandeso. This soul who spoke just now was feeling pride of family, but recognizing that, he has wisely attempted to regain his humility by stating that perhaps I may never have heard of his very famous father.*

The saved soul continued, "I had pride of family. My lineage was ancient, and my ancestors had done notable deeds. I held people in disdain. Because of my disdain, I died. A much larger force besieged my castle. Because I held my enemy in such contempt, I did not surrender, but instead charged into the midst of them, killing many before I myself was killed.

"My name is Omberto. With my death, the power of my family passed on to other people. Because of the pride I had in my family, I now bear this weight on the first ledge of this mountain. I will bear this weight until I have purged my sin and made God happy."

Dante had bent over to listen, and now another soul, also burdened with a stone, lifted his head — with difficulty — enough to look at him and recognize him.

The saved soul called to Dante, who recognized him and said, "You are Oderisi, the artist of Gubbio, who is expert in that art the French call 'Illuminating.' You created artwork in illuminated — that is, illustrated — manuscripts."

Oderisi replied, "Another artist is now better than me. Franco Bolognese illuminates manuscripts with more radiance than I ever did. I had honor, but he has much more honor. When I was alive, however, I would have hated to admit this. I wanted to be the best. I had pride in my talent, and now I carry this stone here. When I was still alive, I turned to God, and I was saved. If not for that, I would be in the Inferno.

"Excessive pride is a sin, and the products of one's pride soon fade. Another artist comes along who is better. Cimabue was once the number-one painter, and now Giotto is known to be superior to him. Guido Guinizelli was once the number-one poet, and now Guido Cavalcanti is known to be superior to him. And perhaps the poet who will surpass Guido Cavalcanti has been born."

Dante, who in the future surpassed Guido Cavalcanti, thought, *I saw Guido Cavalcanti's father in the Inferno. He was in the tomb with Farinata.*

Oderisi continued, "Few people achieve lasting fame. For most people, earthly fame is like a gust of wind. Consider a person who dies in infancy and a person who dies of old age. One thousand years from now, both are likely to have exactly the same amount of Earthly fame: none. Suppose someone achieves a level of fame in which one is remembered for a thousand years. Compared to Eternity, what is a thousand years?"

Dante thought, *Don't write in order to be famous. You need to have a better reason when you write.*

Oderisi continued, "Look at the soul just ahead. At one time everyone in Tuscany spoke about him, but now his name is barely mentioned even in Siena, the city he ruled. At one time, he had so much power that he could advocate that Florence be entirely destroyed. And Florence used to be proud, but now it is like a whore.

"Whatever fame you achieve on Earth will someday fade."

Dante said, "Your words have made me less proud and more humble, but who is the person about whom you were speaking just now?"

Oderisi answered, "His name is Provenzan Salvani."

Dante thought, *Provenzan Salvani is Sienese, like Omberto Aldobrandesco. He is also a famous political figure. He and Farinata, who is in the Inferno, were the victors at the battle of Montaperti in 1260. Provenzan Salvani wanted to destroy Florence following the victory. Farinata, of course, did not want Florence destroyed because he wanted to rule the city. Farinata prevailed in the dispute.*

Oderisi said, "Provenzan Salvani is here because he took pride in his political power. He has been here ever since he died."

Dante said, "Provenzan Salvani delayed repentance until late in life. How was he able to begin climbing immediately? Most souls have to wait the amount of time that they had kept God waiting (unless aided by the sincere prayers of good people). Why didn't God make Provenzan Salvani wait because Provenzan Salvani made God wait?"

Oderisi replied, "At the height of his power, Provenzan Salvani humbled himself. Charles of Anjou was holding one of Provenzan Salvani's friends in prison. Charles declared that he would kill the friend unless the friend was ransomed for 10,000 gold florins. Provenzan Salvani got the money, although he had to beg for it in Siena's marketplace. If anything is a sign of humility, begging is."

Dante the Pilgrim thought, *I can't imagine Farinata begging. He is too proud. I saw him in the Inferno, and he looked like he was posing for a statue.*

Oderisi continued, "Let me make a prophecy. Someday you, Dante, will learn the humility of begging."

Dante the Poet thought, *After I was exiled from Florence, I indeed had to beg for help from others.*

Chapter 12: First Ledge — Exempla of Pride (Purgatory)

Like humble oxen submitting to the yoke, Dante and Oderisi walked together until Virgil said to Dante, "We must move faster, so leave him and press forward. On this mountain, each one must press ahead with all the speed that each one is able to use."

Dante now stood up straight, but his thoughts were still humble. Now Dante and Virgil walked together much more quickly. By spending time on this terrace dedicated to purging the sin of pride, they were becoming lighter of foot.

Virgil said, "Look down. You will see something that you can learn from and that will make your journey up the mountain easier."

Dante looked down and saw carvings of the kind that might be seen on a tomb to preserve the memory of the person whose body is within. Often, such carvings bring tears to the eyes of a pious person who remembers the dead.

These carvings were similar, but of higher artistic quality. Like the previous carvings that were on the side of the mountain, these carvings on the ledge were intended to teach. Previously, the carvings on the side of the mountain taught examples of humility. Now, these carvings on the ledge taught examples of pride.

First in the works of art, Dante saw the angel who was supposed to be the most beautiful of all, the one who rebelled against God and now resides at the bottom of the Inferno, chewing the worst sinners of all time in his three mouths for all time. This angel is Lucifer. Lucifer was so proud that he rebelled against God.

Then in the works of art Dante saw Briareus, who rebelled against Jupiter, the King of gods and men in ancient times. Just as Lucifer tried to unseat God, so Briareus tried to unseat Jupiter, who killed him with a thunderbolt. Briareus and other giants fought against Jupiter and the gods on Olympus. After the battle, Apollo, Minerva, Mars, and Jupiter looked down at the severed and scattered arms and legs of the giants they had defeated. Briareus is now one of the giants who guard the well that leads to the Final Circle of the Inferno. Briareus was so proud that he rebelled against Jupiter.

And in the works of art Dante saw Nimrod, who thought that he could build a tower that would reach Heaven. To stop the tower from being built, God created many languages instead of the one language that human beings had spoken until that time. Because the workers were now speaking different languages, they were unable to coordinate their actions and so the Tower of Babel was not built. Because of Nimrod's pride, God changed the speech of human beings, and now human beings no longer share the same language. Nimrod is another of the giants who guard the well that leads to the Final Circle of the Inferno. Nimrod was so proud that he rebelled against God.

And in the works of art Dante saw Niobe, who had seven sons and seven daughters, and so she boasted that she was more worthy of praise than Latona, aka Leto, who had given birth to only one son and only one daughter: the god Apollo and the goddess Diana. Because of Niobe's pride, Apollo and Diana killed all of Niobe's children in one day. Because of Niobe's pride, Apollo and Diana turned her to stone. Even when she was stone, she grieved for the deaths of her children, and tears trickled down her marble cheeks. Niobe was so proud that she thought she was a better mother than the goddess mother of the god Apollo and goddess Diana.

And in the works of art Dante saw King Saul, the first King of the Israelites. Saul disobeyed a command of God, and after losing a battle to the Philistines, he committed suicide on Mount Gilboa by falling on his sword rather than be captured. After Saul died, David cursed Mount Gilboa with drought. Saul was so proud that he disobeyed a commandment that God made to him.

And in the works of art Dante saw Arachne, who challenged Minerva to a weaving contest. Arachne produced a magnificent cloth without fault, but because of Arachne's pride, Minerva tore up the cloth and turned Arachne into a spider. Arachne was so proud that she challenged the goddess Minerva to a weaving contest.

And in the works of art Dante saw Rehoboam, who arrogantly rejected the advice of wise old men and would not lower the taxes on the tribes of Israel. Rehoboam sent Adoram to collect the exorbitant taxes, the tribes revolted and stoned Adoram to death, and Rehoboam fled, although no one was pursuing him. Rehoboam was so proud that he ignored the advice of wise old men.

And in the works of art Dante saw Alcmeon, who avenged his father, Amphiaraus, a soothsayer who knew that he would die if he took part in a war against Thebes and so hid himself. Polynices, the leader of the forces against Thebes, bribed Eriphyle, the wife of Amphiaraus, with a gold necklace to reveal her husband's hiding place. Forced to go to war against Thebes, Amphiaraus asked Alcmeon to avenge him, and Alcmeon killed his mother, Eriphyle. Alcmeon was so proud that he killed his own mother.

And in the works of art Dante saw the two sons of Sennacherib, the King of Assyria, who warred against the Israelites, who defeated his superior number of forces with divine aid. Later, when Sennacherib was praying to false gods, his two sons murdered him. The two sons of Sennacherib were so proud that they killed their own father.

And in the works of art Dante saw Tomyris, the Queen of a Scythian people, who avenged the death of her son, whom the Persian Emperor Cyrus had murdered. Her army defeated his army, and he died in the battle. Her thirst for revenge was not satisfied by his death, so she cut off his head and threw it into a container that was filled with human blood, saying as she did so, "Drink your fill." Tomyris was so proud that her revenge went beyond the bounds of human decency.

And in the works of art Dante saw the Assyrians who had been led by Holofernes, the general of King Nebuchadnezzar of Babylon. Holofernes attacked the Israelite city Bethulia, and he mocked the god of the Assyrians. Judith, an Israelite heroine, went to Holofernes' tent, gaining entrance by pretending that she would tell him information that would help him conquer the Israelites; however, a few days later when Holofernes lay drunk, she cut off his head with a sword and brought the head back to the Israelites. The next day, learning that Holofernes was dead, the Assyrian army fled. The Assyrians were so proud that they warred against the Israelites and mocked the one true God.

And in the works of art Dante saw the city of Troy. Paris, a prince of Troy, stole Helen, the most beautiful woman in the world, from Menelaus, her lawful husband, in addition to stealing treasure from him. Because of Paris' pride, and because the Trojan citizens would not return Helen to Menelaus, Troy fell to an Achaean army led by Agamemnon, Menelaus' brother. Paris was so proud that he stole the lawfully wedded wife of another man, and the Trojans were so proud that they would not return the wife to her legal husband.

The art that Dante saw on the ledge was much better than the art created by human beings. God had created the art on the ledge. Looking at the art,

Dante thought that the depictions of the living people really seemed to be living people and the depictions of the dead people really seemed to be dead people. No eyewitness to the scenes depicted had a better view of the scenes than Dante.

Dante the Poet thought, *So be proud, sons of Eve, if you dare. If you are proud, hold your head high so that you never look down and see the evils of the pride you regard so highly. If I were asked for a synonym of "man," I would give the answer "pride."*

Dante the Pilgrim kept walking, and thinking, until noon. Then Virgil said to him, "Raise your head now. Look, and see. An angel is coming. Show reverence when you look at the angel so that he will help us. Let us not waste time. We will never see this day again when it is over."

Dante the Pilgrim thought, *Often, you tell me not to waste time. You are correct.*

The angel, wearing white and with his face shining, came to Dante and Virgil. He first spread his arms, and then he spread his wings. He told them, "Come. The steps you must climb are very close. You will find the climbing much easier from here on."

Dante the Poet thought, *Such an invitation is given to all men and women, but few accept it. All men and women should climb high, but for most a little puff of wind keeps them from climbing higher and makes them fall back down.*

The angel led Dante and Virgil to a cleft in the rock, and he brushed his wings against Dante's brow before telling him that his climb would go well.

Climbing upwards was easier in part because the stone had steps. Previously, they had followed a path through a narrow cleft in the rock.

While Dante and Virgil were climbing those steps, they heard sweetly sung a beatitude: "Blessed are the poor in spirit: for theirs is the kingdom of Heaven."

Dante the Pilgrim thought, *Entering a new area of Purgatory is much different from entering a new area of the Inferno. In Purgatory, one hears music; in the Inferno, one hears cries of grief, violently expressed.*

Dante felt light as he climbed the steps. The steps made the climbing easier, but they could not be the full explanation for why he was climbing upward so much easier than before.

Dante asked Virgil, "Why do I feel so light now? Why does climbing up the mountain seem so much easier?"

Virgil replied, "The angel has removed one of the P's from your forehead, and the other P's are much lighter than they were. By purging the sin of pride, which is the foundation of all of the other sins, you are lighter because the burden of pride has been lifted from you. When all of the other P's on your forehead have been completely removed like the first P, you will easily climb upward. Your feet will not complain; instead, they will rejoice."

Dante the Pilgrim, hearing that one of the P's had been removed from his forehead, used his right hand to explore his forehead. Yes, six P's — not seven — were on his forehead. He had six more sins to purge.

Virgil watched as Dante touched his forehead, and Virgil smiled.

Chapter 13: Second Ledge — Envy (Sapia) (Purgatory)

Dante and Virgil reached the next ledge: the second ledge of Purgatory Proper. This terrace was much like the one below it, but because it was higher on the mountain, the circle it made around the mountain was smaller.

Here no souls could be immediately seen. Here no sculpture could be seen. No bas-reliefs were on the wall or ledge of the mountain. The color of the rock was dark like a bruise.

Virgil said, "If we wait until someone comes whom we can ask directions from, we may lose much time."

Virgil looked at the Sun, a symbol of God for many, but a symbol of Natural Reason to Virgil. Natural Reason — what we can learn from reason and from nature — is a good guide that we should follow unless it is superceded by something that is superior to it: Revelation from God.

Virgil prayed to what the Sun represented for him, "Light in whom I place my trust, please guide us. We are unfamiliar with this place, and so we need guidance. You are warm and light the world. We should always look to you unless you are superceded by something that is superior to you."

Dante and Virgil walked along the ledge for a mile — quickly, for they wanted to climb the mountain quickly. Then they began to hear voices without bodies.

The first voice they heard said, "They have no wine," as it flew by them.

Dante thought, *Jesus' very first miracle was turning water into wine so that the guests at a wedding in Cana of Galilee could celebrate. This is a miracle that Jesus performed at the request of his mother, Mary. This shows generosity on the part of Mary. She wanted other people to be able to celebrate a wedding properly. She was concerned with the happiness of other people, and she showed her love for other people.*

Before the sound of the first voice had faded, Dante and Virgil heard another voice cry, "I am Orestes!"

Dante thought, *When Agamemnon returned home to Greece after fighting the Trojan War for 10 years, his wife, Clytemnestra, killed him. She had taken a lover during the years that he was away from home. Her son, Orestes, killed her because she killed his father, and Orestes was sentenced to die. His friend Pylades was willing to die in Orestes' place, although Orestes did not want him to, so both told the executioners, "I am Orestes!" In John 15:13, we read, "Greater love has no man than this, that a man lay down his life for his friends." Pylades loved Orestes so much that he was willing to die for him.*

Dante asked Virgil, "Where are these voices coming from?"

They then heard a third voice: "Love your enemies."

Dante thought, *Matthew 5:44-45 gives us the words of Jesus: "But I say to you, Love your enemies, bless them who curse you, do good to them who hate you, and pray for them who despitefully use you, and persecute you; That you may be the children of your Father who is in Heaven: for He makes His Sun to rise on the evil and on the good, and sends rain on the just and on the unjust."*

Virgil answered Dante's question: "On the second ledge of the Mountain of Purgatory, the envious purge their sin. What you are hearing are examples of the virtues that are opposed to envy: kindness and the love of others. In addition to the examples of the virtue, you will learn examples of the sin itself.

"Now look ahead, and look carefully. Some people are over there; their backs are against the cliff."

Dante looked ahead, and he saw souls wrapped in cloaks that were the color of bruises.

As Dante and Virgil came nearer to these souls, they heard the souls cry, "Holy Mary, pray for us" and "Michael, Peter, and All Saints." The souls were singing the "Litany of the Saints," of which this is a small part:

"Holy Mary, pray for us.

"Holy Mother of God, pray for us.

"Holy Virgin of virgins, pray for us."

Dante the Pilgrim thought, *Any person on Earth would feel pity if he or she saw what I saw. I cried. They looked like blind beggars asking for alms at the doors of churches. They ask for food, and one blind beggar leans against another blind beggar for support. Their cries arouse pity, and simply looking at them arouses pity. Blind people cannot enjoy sunlight, and these saved souls were still denied the light of Heaven until they could climb to the top of the mountain. The eyelids of the envious had been sewn together with iron thread, just as falconers will sew with silken thread the eyelids of falcons to make them quiet and tame them. These souls when living had looked upon their neighbors with envious eyes, and now they can no longer look upon anything. Because they are blind now, voices teach them the virtue of loving others. In life, their sin of envy had bruised their soul, and so now they wear cloaks of coarse cloth that is of the color of bruises. In life, they had wished evil upon their neighbor, but now they lean upon their neighbor for support or give support to their neighbor.*

Dante felt guilty because he was looking at people who could not look at him, and so he turned to Virgil with a question.

Virgil, who could read Dante's mind, answered the question before Dante could ask it: "Yes, you may talk to these souls. Speak briefly, and don't be sidetracked."

Dante was in the middle, between Virgil and the saved souls. Virgil, always protective of Dante, was walking along the outer edge where someone could fall.

Dante said to the souls, "Saved souls, you know that someday you will reach your goal and be in Paradise. Please help me. Is anyone here Italian? I may be of help if someone is."

A saved soul replied, "All of us are citizens of the one true city that is Paradise. You mean to ask if someone here used to be a living person in Italy."

Dante thought, *No destructive factionalism is in Purgatory. Everyone is a citizen of the same place, and everyone helps each other.*

Dante moved forward to where the voice had come and saw a female soul with a raised chin.

Dante asked, "If you are the one who spoke, please tell me your name or tell me where you lived."

The soul replied, "I lived in Siena. Like the others here, I am purging the sin of envy. My name is Sapia, or Wisdom, but I was not wise in life. I enjoyed the discomfort of other people more than the comfort of myself. Listen to a story that shows my lack of wisdom. The men of Siena were fighting a battle outside of the town of Colle. I prayed to God that the Sienese be defeated. The Sienese, led by my nephew Provencal Salvani and by Count Guido Novello, lost the battle, and my nephew, whom I envied for his rise to power, was killed. I rejoiced in the defeat of the Sienese, and I cried to God, "I no longer fear you." I was like a blackbird that is afraid during the cold winter but is cocky during the warm summer.

"I did not repent until at the end of my life. I would still be in Prepurgatory if Peter the Combseller, a good and pious and virtuous man who would not sell a defective comb, had not prayed for me.

"But tell me who you are. If I am correct, your eyelids are not sewn together, and you breathe as you speak."

Dante replied, "Someday my eyes will be sewn shut, but not for long because I seldom look at another person with envy. What fills me with fear is the great amount of time that I will spend on the ledge below that is devoted to purging the sin of pride. Already I seem to be feeling the weight of the stone that I will carry."

Sapia asked, "Who has guided you here? How have you been able to come here if you think to return to a lower ledge?"

Dante replied, "This man beside me who has not spoken is my guide. I am still alive. If you want, once I am back in the Land of the Living I will help you."

Sapia said, "This is a miracle! God really loves you! Yes, please help me. Say a prayer for me occasionally. I also ask you by what you hold valuable to please restore my reputation among my family in Siena. I was envious, but I repented and so I am on this mountain.

"My family lives among foolish people in Siena. The people of Siena are ambitious, but they pursue foolish projects. First they looked in vain for an underground river they named the Diana. Then they embarked upon the more foolish project of building a harbor at Talamone, a project that failed because of malaria and because the harbor filled with silt as quickly as it was dredged."

Chapter 14: Second Ledge — Envy (Guido del Duca, Rinier da Calboli (Purgatory)

Dante heard a saved soul ask another saved soul, "Who is this living man who can open and shut his eyes as he wishes?"

The other saved soul replied, "Who knows? I do know that someone is with him. Why don't you ask nicely who the living man is? If you ask nicely, perhaps he will tell you."

Dante looked at the souls, who raised their heads as if preparing to speak to him.

The first saved soul said, "Living man, who nevertheless is climbing the Mountain of Purgatory, please tell us your name and where you are from. God must love you if He allows you to climb the mountain before you have died. We have never seen that before."

Dante made an effort to be modest and replied, "A little river has its source in Falterona and wanders through Tuscany for over one hundred miles. I come from a city by that river. I need not tell you my name because I am not yet famous."

Virgil thought, *You are making an attempt to be modest, Dante, but you have not fully succeeded. You say that you are* not yet *famous.*

The first saved soul said, "If I have correctly understood you, you are speaking of the Arno River."

The second saved soul asked the first, "Why did he not name the river? It is as if the name of the river is too horrible to say aloud."

The first saved soul said, "I don't know why he did not name the river, but I know that if the name of the valley the river runs through were to die, it would be a blessing. From its source to the place where the river runs into the sea, the inhabitants of the valley the river runs through hate virtue as they hate a snake. The valley may be cursed, or the inhabitants may be affected by the corruption that has long existed, but for whatever reason, the inhabitants have changed their nature. They used to be human beings, but now it is as if they are like Ulysses' men who were transformed into pigs by the sorceress Circe and thereafter lived in sties and ate from troughs.

"This river first flows past the hoggish brutes of Casentino. Instead of eating food prepared for human consumption, they should be eating acorns, a food for pigs.

"Next the river flows past people who are the equivalent of undesirable mongrels who snarl often and bite occasionally. Usually, they snarl and turn away.

"Then the river — or more accurately, the sewer-ditch — flows past Florence, in which exist humans who are more like wolves than dogs.

"And finally the river flows past Pisa, whose inhabitants are like foxes. They are frauds, and they are experts at evading traps.

"I will continue speaking because the spirit of prophecy is upon me. Although you, my companion on this ledge, will feel pain, it is good for you to know my prophecy.

"I see your grandson, Fulcieri da Calboli, cruel and proud and famous for both qualities, committing atrocities against the White Guelfs of Florence. He will hunt the wolves. Through his actions, he will take away their lives and at the same time take away his honor. He is bloody."

The second saved soul grieved. He was not envious of the inhabitants of Florence: He did not rejoice in their pain and death, and he did not rejoice in Fulcieri's evil.

Dante was curious about these two saved souls, and so he asked them for their names.

The first saved soul replied, "Although you declined to tell me your name when I asked for it, I will tell you our names because God has honored you. I am Guido del Duca. I was envious, and I hated to see the happiness of another person. I sowed envy; now I reap purgation. Now I wonder why Humankind wants those things that either cannot be shared or are lesser when they are shared instead of wanting those things that are greater when they are shared.

"The saved soul beside me is Rinier da Calboli, whom Guido da Montefeltro defeated in battle in 1276. He has no heirs to inherit his very great worth. Throughout the entire region of Romagna, many families are lacking good and chivalrous people. All who remain are evil.

"Where are the good people of Romagna? Dead. Gone.

"Where are Mainardi, Lizio da Valbona, and Pier Traversaro?

"Where is Guido di Carpigna, who was so hospitable that he once sold half of a valuable quilt in order to pay for a banquet, saying that all he needed was half a quilt because in winter he slept curled up and in summer he did not cover his feet?

"Where are Fabbro de' Lambertazzi, Bernardo di Fosco, Ugolin d'Azzo, Guido da Prata, Federigo di Tignoso, members of the Traversaro clan, and members of the Anastagi clan? These two clans have no heirs.

"Where are these people? They were models of chivalry and virtue, but they are no more.

"Which people exist now? Only the bad.

"Bretinoro is a town in Romagna that ought to no longer exist because no longer do good people live in it. It is best that families in this town have no sons. The heirs of families in this town are degenerate. Only families with no sons have a chance of retaining the goodness of their name.

"But now, living man from Tuscany who is climbing the mountain by the will of God, continue your journey. I am so disgusted by the degeneracy of the inhabitants of Romagna that I need to cry rather than to speak."

Dante thought, *Guido del Duca has come a long way in being purged of the sin of envy. Envious people are saddened when other people have good fortune, and they are made happy when other people have bad fortune. If Guido were still envious, he would be happy at the bad fortune of living people — being evil is bad fortune because evil people run the risk of eternal damnation unless they repent.*

Virgil thought, *Guido del Duca has come a long way in being purged of the sin of envy. Guido is not envious of Dante, to whom God is showing special grace by allowing him to travel through Purgatory although he is still alive.*

Dante and Virgil walked away. The saved souls were silent, and so Dante and Virgil knew that they were traveling in the right direction. If they had gone in the wrong direction, the saved souls would have told them. Souls in Purgatory are helpful.

As Dante and Virgil walked, they heard a voice say, "Anyone who finds me shall slay me."

Dante thought, *According to the Biblical story of Cain and Abel, both brothers gave offerings to God. Cain was a farmer, and his offering was "the fruit of the ground." Abel was a shepherd, and his offering was "the firstlings of his flock and the fat thereof." God liked Abel's offering, but God did not like Cain's offering.*

Out of envy, Cain killed Abel. Of course, God knew that Cain had killed Abel, and God punished Cain by sending him into exile. Cain then said the words that appear here in Purgatory: "Anyone who finds me shall slay me." However, God is merciful, and He marked Cain as a sign that no one should kill him. Cain was so envious of Abel that he killed him.

Then Dante and Virgil heard another voice: "I am Aglauros, and I was turned to stone."

Dante thought, *I have read this story in Ovid's* Metamorphoses. *Aglauros was envious of her sister, whom the god Mercury loved. Aglauros attempted to keep Mercury from seeing her sister, and Mercury turned her into a stone statue.*

Virgil said to Dante, "You have just heard two examples of people infected with envy. Learn from them why envy must be avoided. Too often, Humankind gives in to sin, and neither positive examples of virtues nor negative examples of sins educate them and affect their actions. Paradise is above, but Humankind looks below. God is aware, and God strikes down those who focus their attention on the wrong place."

Chapter 15: Third Ledge — Anger (Purgatory)

The time was 3 p.m. — the Sun is never still just as a child running and playing is never still — when Dante saw a light that was brighter than any that he had previously seen. His mind was stunned, and his head was forced down, and he put his hands above his head in an unsuccessful attempt to shield himself from the light.

Dante asked Virgil, "What light is this? I can't shield myself from it! Isn't it moving toward us?"

Virgil replied, "Don't be surprised that the brightness of angels can still blind you. We are being invited to climb to the next ledge of the mountain. Soon, you will be able to look at angels and see them without being blinded. The more that you are without sin, the more that you will be able to see."

Dante and Virgil stood before the angel, who said, "Climb higher now. These stairs are less steep than the stairs you have climbed before. The more that you are without sin, the easier it will be for you to climb."

Dante and Virgil walked past the angel and started climbing, and they heard the angel sing, "Blessed are the merciful: for they shall obtain mercy." They also heard "Conquer and rejoice." Having conquered another sin, they rejoiced.

Dante wished to learn from Virgil as they climbed, so he asked, "What did Guido del Luca mean when he said, 'Now I wonder why Humankind wants those things that either cannot be shared or are lesser when they are shared instead of wanting those things that are greater when they are shared'?"

Virgil replied, "He wishes you to avoid his sin: envy. He wishes you not to strive for material things but instead to strive for things that are nonmaterial."

Dante asked, "Can you explain in more detail, and give some examples?"

Virgil said, "Those things that are lesser when they are shared are material things. If you have $100 and you pay someone $50 to perform a task for you, you have only $50 left. What was once $100 is now $50. That can lead you to become envious of someone who has $100.

"Here is another example: Suppose you have a rare book that is worth $1,000. If you own it by yourself, you have the equivalent of $1,000. But if you are an equal co-owner of it with someone else, then you have the equivalent of $500. Material possessions, when shared, become lesser. Often, of course, material possessions are not shared. When it comes to material possessions, if one person owns something, then other people do not own it."

Dante asked, "How can something that is shared by many souls make each of those souls wealthier?"

Virgil replied, "Nonmaterial, and especially spiritual, things, when shared, become greater. For example: Instead of owning a valuable and rare edition of a good book, suppose you and a friend both read an inexpensive edition of that good book. What you would share would be an appreciation and knowledge of the book. This is something that can be shared by all the people who read that book. When that is shared, it becomes greater, not lesser.

"The more someone loves God, the more they are able to know that God loves him or her. Beatrice told me that in Paradise everybody shares his or her spiritual gifts, and everybody gains because of the sharing.

"Love is shared and grows greater in Paradise, and Paradise is what you should strive for.

"If my words are hard to understand, soon you will see Beatrice, and she can help you to truly understand.

"For right now, work to rid yourself of the five P's that remain on your forehead. Two have entirely vanished. The angel brushed your forehead with his wings and erased a second P."

Dante was going to say, "I understand," but he was distracted because he and Virgil had reached the next ledge.

Here Dante fell into a trance, and he saw visions. These were visions of Meekness and Patience, the virtues opposed to the sin of Wrath.

The first vision was of Mary asking her young son, Jesus, "Why have you treated us in this way? Your father and I, frightened and crying, have searched throughout Jerusalem to find you." Mary, Joseph, and Jesus had gone to Jerusalem for Passover. When Joseph and Mary left Jerusalem, they assumed that Jesus was in the group of people, including kinsmen and friends, with whom they were traveling. They traveled an entire day and discovered that Jesus was not in their group of people. They returned to Jerusalem and spent three days searching for him before finding him teaching in a temple. All parents would be relieved to find their lost child, and most parents would then be understandably angry at the child for causing them to worry that the child had died or been injured or been kidnapped. But Mary did not get angry at Jesus. She simply asked, "Why have you treated us in this way?"

The second vision was of a kind ruler of Athens, Pisistratus, who was known for his ability to deal with angry people. His wife, crying, was upset because a young man had publicly hugged their daughter, and so she wanted him killed. She said to her husband the King, "Since you are the ruler of Athens, take vengeance on this man who hugged our daughter." In reply, Pisistratus asked her, "What shall we do to those who want to harm us, if we condemn those who love us?" Pisistratus felt compassion for, not anger toward, the young man.

The third vision was of Saint Stephen, the first Christian martyr, who died while praying for the forgiveness of his killers. The attackers were throwing stones at him and crying, "Kill him! Kill him!" But Stephen cried, "Lord, lay not this sin to their charge." Even as he died, Stephen forgave his enemies and wished that God would show them mercy.

Dante recognized that these were visions and were not actually happening in front of him, but he recognized the truth that resided in the visions.

Virgil saw that Dante had finished experiencing the visions, and he asked Dante, "What is wrong with you? You have been walking unsteadily, as if you are half-asleep."

Dante replied, "I will tell you the visions I have seen."

Virgil replied, "I know every thought you had. I know the visions you have seen. They were given to you so that you may learn from them and may learn to avoid the sin of anger and instead enjoy the peace that comes from Paradise.

"When I asked, 'What's wrong with you?' after the visions had ceased, I simply wanted to encourage you to move faster. Those who climb the mountain must not be lazy. Here vigor is needed."

Dante and Virgil walked together, and a cloud of black smoke rose and moved toward them. It enveloped them and they were not able to see. The smoke also made the air noxious.

Chapter 16: Third Ledge — Anger (Marco Lombard) (Purgatory)

No night was ever so dark as the darkness created by the smoke that enveloped Dante and Virgil. No veil ever obscured vision as much as that smoke.

The smoke was so stinging that Dante could not see, and so Virgil grabbed Dante's hand. Virgil placed Dante's hand on his shoulder so he could be Dante's guide through the smoke. Virgil was a sighted man leading a blind man.

Virgil told Dante, "Be careful not to go away from me. You need me now."

Dante thought, *That is true in more than one sense. I literally need Virgil to prevent me from going over the edge of this ledge of the mountain. But also Virgil is a perfect example of reason. This smoke is blinding me the way that anger can blind a human being. Reason is needed to be a guide to good conduct when one is angry. If a human being is not guided by reason, that human being can do harmful actions.*

Dante heard voices singing the "*Agnus Dei*" or the "Lamb of God":

"Lamb of God, You who take away the sins of the world,

"Have mercy on us.

"Lamb of God, You who take away the sins of the world,

"Grant us peace."

The voices sang the song in unison and harmony.

Dante asked Virgil, "Those voices — do they come from saved souls?"

Virgil replied, "Yes. The lyrics help heal and take away anger."

One of the saved souls then spoke: "Who are you who walks through the smoke? You are speaking of us saved souls as if you were not one of us — as if you were still living and measuring time by the calendar instead of by the intensity of your purgation."

Dante replied, "Saved soul, you who clean your soul so you can give it back to God, I can tell you wonders if you walk with me."

Dante thought, *The wonders are that I have traveled through the Inferno and am climbing this mountain although I am still alive.*

The saved soul replied, "I will walk with you for a while — for as long as I am allowed. Because of this smoke, we cannot see each other's face, but we can hear each other's words."

Dante said, "I am still alive, and God is allowing me to climb this mountain. To get to the Mountain of Purgatory, I journeyed through the Inferno.

"God wants me to see Paradise. Please tell me who you are, and please tell me the way up this mountain. We will follow your instructions so that we may climb higher."

The saved soul replied, "My name is Marco, and I come from Lombard. I knew the world, each of whose inhabitants is like a slackened bow that no one uses to aim at virtue. The path you are on is the correct one; it will lead to the way up to the next ledge. When you are above, in Paradise, please pray for me."

Dante replied, "I promise that I will pray for you, just as you have requested. But I have a question that I hope you can answer. This has been bothering me. As you have said, correctly, the world lacks every virtue and it lacks no evil. Why? Please tell me so that I can tell living men. Some people believe that the cause of evil is due to the stars' and planets' influence on people, while other people think that the cause of evil is people themselves."

Marco sighed and said, "The world is blind, and from your question I can see that in this matter you are blind, too. Too many people on earth attribute evil entirely to the influence of the stars and planets on people. If this were true, human beings would have no Free Will. And if people have no Free Will, why should people be rewarded with the bliss of Paradise for doing good or rewarded with the pain of the Inferno for doing evil?

"If Free Will does not exist, then God's afterlife does not make sense. Why should there be an Inferno if people are not responsible for their sins? Why should there be a Paradise if people are not responsible for their good deeds? Why should there be a Purgatory if people are not responsible for the sins they have repented and are not responsible for their repentance? If no Free Will exists, people are not responsible for what they do or don't do.

"But first let me give you some background information. People of your time and my time believed in the astrological idea that the stars and planets influence us. People in the afterlife are often able to see the future. I see that the future will bring the rise of science, which will show that the stars and planets do not influence us. Astrology is not science. However, it is true that heredity — as well as environment — influence us. Instead of the influence of the stars and the planets, we should talk about the influence of heredity and environment. And neither the influence of heredity nor the influence of environment takes away our Free Will. People still know the difference between good and evil, and people still have the ability to choose to do good or chose to do evil.

"According to Determinism, nothing is free to move in any other way than it moves. Everything follows natural laws. For example, planets orbit the Sun because of natural laws. Planets are not free to stop orbiting the Sun. Planets are not free to stop revolving. We will never have a day in which the Earth stops revolving for an entire day, meaning that one side of the planet is light for 24 hours, and the other side is dark for 24 hours, and then the planet starts revolving again. Using the laws of physics, scientists will be able to accurately predict where a planet will be 100 years from now.

"Of course, Determinism as applied to planets is not controversial. However, people who are Determinists say that human beings are also determined. We are alive, however, and therefore it is much more difficult to predict our behavior, but according to the Determinists, everything we do is caused by our environment and heredity. According to the Determinists, Humankind does not have Free Will. Whenever we make a decision, we are making the decision in accordance with the kind of character we have. Our character is caused by heredity and environment. According to the Determinists, we have no Free Will that we can use to shape our character.

"In contrast, Free Will is what it sounds like. Planets may be determined, but human beings have the ability to make choices. You can choose to do good, or you can choose to do evil. The choice is yours to freely make.

"Human beings are free to choose good or evil, and so if the world is filled with moral evil, that is due to human beings alone, and not due to heredity, with an exception given to the criminally insane, who, like criminals, should be locked up, although the criminally insane should be locked up in a mental hospital rather than a prison.

"Just because you have Free Will does not mean that it is easy to use it. Doing the right thing can mean making a major effort of the will. Willing yourself to do the right thing can be difficult.

"Instead of you giving in to your desires and saying that what you do is determined by the planets and stars (or by heredity and environment), you need to work at controlling your desires. Instead of taking the easy way out and giving in to every desire, you need to decide what it is that you ought to do, and then you need to do it.

"This is something that all of us ought to be working for. In fact, it is what the souls in Purgatory are working for. Instead of giving in to feelings of anger, or envy, or pride, the souls in Purgatory want to rein in these feelings and to substitute instead feelings of meekness, generosity, and humility.

"Listen, for this is important. I will explain to you how evil enters the world. The soul is born innocent, without evil. The soul can turn its attention to various things, some of which can be as trivial as a toy. The soul needs good guidance. The soul needs good teachers, just laws, and good rulers. We need good lawmakers to come up with just laws to be a guide for us. The just laws will not annihilate our excessive desires, but just laws can help us restrain our excessive desires.

"Currently, Italy has good laws, but it has no one to enforce them. The Holy Roman Emperor is not in Italy, and the current Pope, Boniface VIII, is more interested in playing power politics than in ruling justly and enforcing just laws, so the Roman law is not doing Italy any good. The Holy Roman Emperor and the Pope have even fought each other instead of working together to provide a good environment for all people, including the common people.

"The people who should be enforcing just laws are instead more interested in gaining wealth and power. The bad behavior of their leaders has a bad influence on the common people.

"Yes, we do have Free Will, but it is best not to be tempted in the first place. Bad leaders can create a society in which temptation reigns.

"Bad leadership has created an environment in which it is difficult for people to use their Free Will to do the right thing. The Pope and the Bishops are pursuing wealth and power. The common people see that, and they feel free to pursue their own base desires. Just leadership is important if you want a just society.

"Three good people still exist: Currado da Palazzo, "Three good people still exist: Currado da Palazzo, Gherardo da Camino (who was the captain-general of Treviuso and the father of Gaia, a poet), and the nobleman and poet Guido da Castel. Currado bore a banner in a battle. Even though both of his hands were cut off, he held the banner in his arms and kept it waving to boost the morale of the troops.

"Dante, tell the world that the Pope has grabbed secular power as well as spiritual power. Secular power does not belong to the Pope."

Dante replied, "Well spoken, Marco. I see why the sons of Levi were not permitted to inherit wealth. They served the Temple, and to keep focused on their service, they were not permitted to own property. The Pope and the Church have amassed secular power and wealth and so are distracted from the spiritual service that they should be performing."

Marco said, "Rays of light are piercing the smoke. We are approaching the angel. I must leave before the angel sees me. God be with you."

Marco turned and walked away from Dante and Virgil.

Dante thought, *I have learned from you, Marco. When I return to the Land of the Living, I must be a good leader. Leaders need not be Emperors or Popes; they can be teachers, parents, and other ordinary people, including poets.*

I have also learned that Free Will exists and that we ought not to blame the stars and planets for our actions. Astrologers do that, and astrologers are in the Inferno.

Suppose you regarded astrology as a way to live your life. What then? Then you would regard the stars as exerting control over your life. You would not make an important decision without consulting an astrological chart, and then you would decide in accordance with what the stars "told" you.

By doing this, of course, you would be denying your Free Will. You would be controlled by what you think the stars are telling you. A strong belief in astrology can lead to a denial of Free Will. A denial of Free Will can lead to an abdication of responsibility. Repenting your sins means acknowledging that you are responsible for committing sins and regretting your sins. Unless you take responsibility for your sins, you cannot repent your sins. Unless you repent your sins, you cannot achieve Paradise.

The astrologers are in the Inferno because they have kept people from taking responsibility for their actions, including their sins. Sinners can say, "It's no wonder I sinned. The stars predetermine it all. It is not up to me whether or not I sin. Therefore, I don't have to take responsibility for my sins."

Of course, we have seen that many of the sinners in the Inferno avoided taking responsibility for their sins. Francesca da Rimini blamed Love and a book for her sins.

Unless you take responsibility for your actions, how can you change your life for the better?

We need to reject astrology and to affirm Free Will and responsibility.

Chapter 17: Fourth Ledge — Sloth (Purgatory)

Imagine being caught in a mountain fog. Imagine trying to see through the fog with eyes that seem to be covered with membranes, partially blinding you. Imagine that the fog begins to dissipate, and finally you can see the Sun again.

That is how Dante felt as he saw the Sun again, just before the Sun set.

Following Virgil, Dante walked out of the cloud of thick smoke that blinded the wrathful. Similar to how he had experienced examples of meekness, now he experienced examples of wrath — in inner visions.

Where do such inner visions come from? Some people say from the stars; other people say from God. The people who say that the inner visions experienced on the Mountain of Purgatory come from God are correct.

First, Dante experienced an inner vision of Procne, a wrathful woman who was transformed into a bird in a myth told in Book 6 of Ovid's *Metamorphoses*. Procne was married to Tereus, a Thracian King, and she bore him a son named Itys. Tereus then raped Procne's sister, Philomela, and cut out her tongue so that she could not tell anyone what had happened. Philomela wove a tapestry. The tapestry contained pictures that told the story of the rape. When Procne saw the tapestry and realized that her husband had raped her sister, she was so angry that she killed her son, cooked him, and served him to her husband.

Procne experienced anger against family.

Second, Dante experienced an inner vision of the Persian Haman, a high official of the Persian King Ahasuerus, who is better known in modern times as Xerxes. He was famous in ancient Greek history as well as in Old Testament history. In ancient Greek history, his father, Darius, invaded the Greek mainland, but was defeated at Marathon. People got the name "marathon" for our long-distance race because a runner carried the news of the Greek victory all the way to Athens, dying after he delivered the news. Xerxes also invaded the Greek mainland. He was delayed at Thermopylae, a pass in the mountains. During the Battle of Thermopylae, 300 Spartans, and 1000 other Greeks, led by King Leonidas of Sparta, held off the vastly numerically superior Persians for a few days, giving the Greeks time to gather their forces. The Spartans knew that they would die. King Leonidas told them that they would eat the morning meal in the Land of the Living, and they would eat the evening meal in the Land of the Dead. The Greeks defeated the Persians in such battles as the Battle of Salamis and the Battle of Plataea, thus preventing the Persians from subjugating Greece.

According to the Book of Esther in the Bible, Haman decided to have all the Jews killed because Mordecai, the cousin of Esther, would not bow down to him. Haman told Xerxes that some people in his kingdom did not obey his laws, and therefore those people ought to be killed. Xerxes agreed.

Esther asked that the Jews, herself included, fast for three days, and then she would see the King. (She was his Queen.) Xerxes was unable to sleep one night, and he ordered a book of chronicles to be read to him. The selection read told about the loyalty of Mordecai, who had prevented a plot to assassinate King Xerxes by two eunuchs.

Esther went to King Xerxes, her husband, and asked him not to kill all the Jews. He asked who was planning to kill all the Jews. Hearing from Esther that Haman was planning to kill all the Jews, Xerxes ordered that Haman be crucified. In fact, the crucifix that Haman had planned to use to crucify Mordecai was used to crucify Haman. Even as Haman died, he was still filled with anger against Mordecai.

Haman experienced anger against neighbor.

Third, Dante experienced an inner vision of Queen Amata, who committed suicide. Virgil's *Aeneid* tells her story. Amata, a Queen in Italy, wanted her daughter, Lavinia, to marry Turnus. However, following the end of the Trojan War, the Trojan Prince Aeneas came to Italy in order to fulfill his fate of becoming an important ancestor of the Roman people. Aeneas was fated to marry Lavinia, and together they would have children and their descendants would eventually become the Romans. Turnus wanted to marry Lavinia, and he fought a war against Aeneas and the Trojan warriors whom Aeneas had brought with him.

When Queen Amata heard a rumor — it turned out to be false — that Turnus had been killed in battle, she committed suicide rather than see Lavinia married to Aeneas. Lavinia mourned when she discovered that her mother was dead. Lavinia said, "Why, mother, did you allow your rage to take away your life? Now I must mourn you before I mourn another person who will soon die — Turnus!"

Queen Amata experienced anger against God — who wanted Aeneas to marry Lavinia and become an important ancestor of the Roman people.

A person who is asleep will wake up when light suddenly falls across his or her eyes. So Dante woke up when bright light flashed across his eyes.

Then Dante heard a voice that said, "This is the place where you can climb higher."

Virgil explained, "This is an angel. Very helpful, he tells us what we need to know even before we ask. He follows the ethical rule 'Treat others as you would like to be treated.' Some people see a person who needs something, but they wait to be asked for help. Such people are half-guilty of not helping those who need help.

"Let us climb as high as we can while light still remains. Once the light is gone, we will not be permitted — or able — to climb higher."

Dante and Virgil started climbing the stairs, and with his first step, Dante felt a wing pass over his forehead, and he heard the words "Blessed are the peacemakers, who feel no sinful wrath."

The light faded, and Dante thought to himself, *Why is my strength fading?*

Dante and Virgil climbed the last of the stairs to the next ledge. Then they stopped, just like a ship has to stop once it runs aground.

Virgil thought, *The end of the day has arrived, and on the Mountain of Purgatory, no sinner can ascend at night.*

Dante listened, heard nothing, and then asked Virgil, "What sin is purged on this ledge? Although we cannot climb higher, we can talk to each other."

Virgil replied, "The sinners here are purging the sin of sloth. They failed to pursue with zeal the things they should have pursued with zeal. The sinners were not necessarily lazy, except when it came to spiritual things. Some sinners here were very busy indeed, just not when it came to pursuing what they should have been pursuing. On this ledge, the sinners pursue with zeal and diligence the purgation of the sin of sloth."

Virgil thought, *I am not a Christian, but I learned much during the Harrowing of Hell. I have also spent much time in the library in Limbo. Beatrice also told me much.*

Virgil continued, "Let me tell you some of what I know about the sins purged on the Mountain of Purgatory. You can benefit from that knowledge.

"All people have love. Love is of two kinds: natural love and rational love. These terms come from Aristotle.

"Natural love is simply a desire for something. Natural love does not involve the use of reason. Later, I will talk about natural love. Right now, I will talk about rational love.

"Rational love involves choosing what we love. One way to look at it is rational love involves choosing what we pursue. We may choose wisely or foolishly. We may choose to pursue what we love with not enough force or with too much force or with just the right amount of force.

"Because we have Free Will, we can choose what we love, and we can choose with how much force we will pursue it. It is important to choose to love the right things and to pursue them with the right amount of force.

"What we choose is what we love. We can choose to love the right thing or the wrong thing.

"Rational love should stay fixed on the Eternal Good. However, we can choose to love the wrong thing, such as money, instead. Or we can choose to love something good but pursue it with either too much zeal or not enough zeal. Making the wrong choice or pursuing what you love with the wrong amount of force can put you in the Inferno or make you spend additional years in Purgatory, depending on whether or not you repent your sins before you die.

"The first three ledges of the Mountain of Purgatory purge the sins of pride, envy, and wrath. These are sins of loving the wrong thing.

"Sinners who were guilty of pride, envy, or wrath were guilty of loving the wrong things; they wished some kind of evil upon their neighbors.

"If a sinner was proud, the sinner placed the sinner at the center of the universe and therefore wished for the sinner's neighbors to be beneath the sinner.

"If a sinner was envious, the sinner placed the sinner at the center of the universe and therefore did not want the sinner's neighbors to have good fortune.

"If a sinner was angry, then the sinner placed the sinner at the center of the universe and therefore wished to do something like punch the sinner's neighbors in the nose.

"We are now on the middle ledge, which purges the sin of sloth. The saved souls here loved the right thing, but they pursued it without sufficient zeal.

"We have three ledges above this ledge to climb. They are devoted to purging the sins that involve loving the right thing too much. I won't tell you what they are. I prefer that you discover for yourself what they are."

Virgil thought, *The ledges above punish the sins of avarice, gluttony, and lust.*

Rational love and staying fixed on the Eternal Good involve staying temperate, something that many unrepentant sinners in the Inferno and many repentant sinners on the Mountain of Purgatory did not do.

Sinners who were guilty of avarice, gluttony, or lust were guilty of loving the right things too much.

If a sinner was guilty of avarice, the sinner loved money or material things too much. The sinner either hoarded money or spent every penny the sinner could borrow in order to get more stuff. Nothing is wrong with money or material possessions provided they are used wisely, but a person can love either money or material possessions too much.

If a sinner was guilty of gluttony, then the sinner over-ate and over-drank. Of course, food and drink are good things if they are used wisely, but the sinner loved food and drink too much.

If a sinner was guilty of lust, then the sinner loved sex too much. God invented sex, and when sex is indulged in wisely and ethically, it is one of the best things on Earth, but it is possible to love sex too much and to misuse sex.

Everyone loves, but it is necessary to love the right things and to love them with the right amount of zeal.

Chapter 18: Fourth Ledge — Sloth (Abbot of San Zeno) (Purgatory)

When Virgil had finished speaking, he looked at Dante to see if he wanted more information. Dante, although he wanted more information, wondered whether Virgil was tired of answering questions. Of course, Virgil could read his mind, and he encouraged him to ask questions.

Dante said, "The information you have given me is very good, but please explain love to me. It is, you say, the source of every virtue as well as of every vice."

Virgil replied, "Listen carefully, and I will explain love. Not every love is good. The Epicureans believed that, but they were wrong. The Epicureans taught something false, and when they taught it, they were like blind people leading other blind people.

"People have desires, but not all desires are good. The Epicureans would say that anything that gives pleasure is good, but the Epicureans are wrong. As we have seen, it is important to love the right things. Loving the wrong things leads to pride, envy, and wrath. It is important to love to the right degree. People who are guilty of sloth love the right things, but not strongly enough. And when we climb to the final three terraces, you will see saved souls who loved the right things but too strongly.

"The soul senses something, whether material or nonmaterial, forms an image of it, and if the image seems desirable, the soul desires — or loves — the thing as naturally as a flame shoots upwards. If the thing is sufficiently desirable, the soul moves toward possessing it."

Dante asked, "If all of this is completely natural, does it make sense for one to be praised or blamed for one's choices, whether good or bad? It seems as if the soul must act as it does."

Virgil replied, "I will explain to you what I can explain. Although the soul's wanting a thing is completely natural, as natural as a bee's making honey, people must use their reason to determine whether to pursue the thing or not. Some things we should pursue, and some things we ought not to pursue. Humankind has knowledge of right and wrong. Humankind has reason. Humankind has ethics. All of these things can help people to decide whether what the soul wants is good or bad. And Humankind has Free Will to make a decision and act on it. Whatever your heredity and environment are, reason can help you make the correct decision and Free Will can help you implement that correct decision.

"We human beings do have Free Will to choose, and what we choose is important.

"To summarize: What we choose is what we love. However, we have reason, and we can use our reason to understand the difference between good loves and bad loves. We also have Freedom of the Will, and we can use our Freedom of the Will to choose good loves.

"I have explained to you what I can explain. When you see Beatrice, she can give you more information. Beatrice, not I, understands faith.

"Intellect will not solve all of our problems or tell us everything that we ought to know. We have had an intellectual discussion of love, but you still need to have faith as well as intellect.

"I understand human reason, but Beatrice understands faith, and Beatrice will be able to take you further than I can.

"Again: Quite simply, intellect is not able to understand everything. Some things will remain a mystery and must be accepted on faith.

"I am aware of my limits, and I am aware that Beatrice will be able to answer some questions that I am unable to answer. I, of course, will soon turn you over to Beatrice. Beatrice will be your next major guide."

The time was close to midnight. Dante was satisfied that Virgil had answered his question the best he was able to, but he realized that Beatrice could answer his question in more detail.

Dante's thoughts began to wander, but then he and Virgil heard people running toward them. The followers of Bacchus in Thebes were zealous in their worship of the god, and the saved souls running toward Dante and Virgil were also zealous.

Two souls were ahead of the others. One soul shouted, "Mary ran to the hills."

Dante thought, *After the Annunciation, in which an angel told Mary that she would bear Christ, Mary hurried to visit her cousin, Elizabeth, who was pregnant with John the Baptist. Mary did not delay; she wished to hurry to share the good news with Elizabeth.*

The next soul shouted, "Caesar struck at Marseilles and then hurried to Spain to subjugate Ilerda."

Dante thought, *Julius Caesar warred against Pompey the Great. Eager to meet Pompey in battle, Caesar left some of his army to besiege Marseilles, and then he took as quickly as he could the rest of his soldiers to the showdown with the Spanish army of Pompey. Caesar won the Battle of Ilerda.*

Mary and Julius Caesar are examples of zeal and diligence that we ought to emulate.

Other souls running behind the two souls in front shouted, "Faster! Faster! Don't waste time! Purge the sin of sloth! Do good deeds to rid yourself of sloth and be blessed!"

Virgil said to the running souls, "Saved souls who are eager to make up for lost time — time lost due to the lukewarm love of doing the right thing and of doing good deeds — this man who is alive would like to climb higher when dawn arrives. Please show us the way up."

One of the saved souls shouted to him, "Follow in our tracks, and you will arrive at the way up the mountain.

"We cannot stop. We cannot lose time. We are keeping our eyes on the prize. We beg your pardon, but we must purge our sin of sloth."

Dante thought, *These souls certainly are keeping their eyes on the prize. Elsewhere on the mountain, souls have been distracted from the prize when they have found out that I am still alive. These souls refuse to be distracted. Cato would be proud of them. Those who were slothful while they were alive are now purging their sin by staying busy day and night. The slothful purge their sin by running and running, both day and night.*

The saved soul continued, "I was the abbot of San Zeno in Verona when Barbarossa was Emperor. He destroyed Milan in 1162, even sowing salt into the ground so that nothing would grow in the fields. A person who has power over the monastery, but who will soon die, replaced the true pastor with a person who is an illegitimate bastard, unqualified mentally because of mental retardation, and unqualified physically because of physical handicaps. Thus, he is triply unqualified. Unless exceptional circumstances exist, a man with these qualities cannot become a priest. Such qualities can interfere with the duties of a priest. For example, a priest with severe physical handicaps may not be able to pour the liquid for the Mass. Living men abuse their power, and they make bad times worse by providing bad leaders."

He raced on.

Virgil said to Dante, "Turn around. More souls are racing toward us as they work to purge the sin of sloth."

Two souls at the end of the group of souls shouted, "Most followers of Moses never reached the Holy Land."

Most of the followers of Moses never reached the Promised Land because they were slothful after God opened the Red Sea so that they could escape from Egypt. As recorded in Numbers 14:22, God told Moses, "Because all those men who have seen my glory, and my miracles, which I did in Egypt and in the wilderness, and have tempted me now these ten times, and have not hearkened to my voice, surely they shall not see the land which I sware unto their fathers, neither shall any of them who provoked me see it." Among the older men, only Joshua the son of Nun, and Caleb the son of Jephunneh, made it to the Holy Land.

And then the two souls at the end shouted, "Some followers of Aeneas never made it to Italy."

Dante thought, *This is true. When Aeneas and his followers were on the island of Sicily, the women set fire to some ships because they were tired of wandering and wanted to stay on Sicily. Some of the ships burned, and Aeneas did not have enough ships to take all of the Trojan refugees to Italy. Therefore, he left nearly all of the women on Sicily (he did take to Italy at least one mother) and all the men who desired to stay there rather than going on to glory in Italy. Virgil tells this story in Book 5 of his* Aeneid.

These slothful followers of Moses and of Aeneas are not to be emulated.

When the souls had gone on, Dante's thoughts wandered. He went to sleep, and he began to dream.

Chapter 19: Fifth Ledge — Avarice and Wastefulness (Purgatory)

Just before dawn, a time when dreams sometimes bring truth, Dante dreamed about a hag — a stutterer and stumbler, with crossed eyes, yellow skin, and hands deformed as if by arthritis. Dante stared at her, and under his gaze the hag changed and became gradually beautiful.

The now beautiful woman spoke, "I am a Siren. I am she who sings sweetly and entices sailors to crash their ships upon my shores. I am the Siren who convinced Ulysses to stray from his path. Anyone who spends time with me seldom leaves because I satisfy them."

Ulysses sought dangerous knowledge. In Homer's *Odyssey*, Circe told him about his upcoming voyage, "First you will come to the island of the Sirens, who enchant men with their lovely song. Sailors who hear their song crash their ships on the Sirens' island, whose shores are strewn with the bones of men. Sail quickly past the Sirens! Your men must not hear their song. Soften beeswax and plug their ears with it. But if you must hear their song, have your men tie you to the mast so that you don't jump overboard and swim to their island and die. Tell your men that when you order them to untie you, they must tie you tighter." Ulysses did this, and he heard the song of the Sirens and lived.

The Siren had barely finished speaking before a Heavenly lady appeared to defend Dante and said to Virgil, "What is this? Do your duty!"

Virgil then stepped up the Siren and ribbed her garment from the top to below her belly. A stench then poured forth, and Dante gagged and woke up.

Virgil said, "I have been calling you three times now. You are slothful, and you are not acting like the saved souls purging their sin on this ledge."

Dante followed Virgil.

As Dante walked, he was thinking about his dream. He was stooped over and resembled half of a bridge. He then heard a soft, kindly voice say, "This is the way up."

An angel's wings fanned Dante and erased one of the remaining P's on his forehead, and the angel said, "Blessed are they who mourn: for they shall be comforted."

Virgil asked Dante, "What are you thinking about?"

Dante replied, "I had a dream that I cannot stop thinking about."

Virgil knew Dante's thoughts, and he knew the dream that Dante had had. He said to Dante, "You saw an evil witch that causes the sinners on the three upper ledges to mourn. You also saw how to escape from her.

"The Siren was once hideous but then seemed beautiful, just as a sin is repulsive at first but when habitually engaged in seems attractive. Think of addiction to tobacco, which a later age will regard as at least a bad habit. Anyone smoking a first cigarette is likely to have a very unpleasant experience, with coughing and, in some cases, vomiting. But continued smoking makes a person an addict to tobacco, and smoking becomes a pleasure — until it results in disease. But a better example is perhaps food. Food is necessary and eating too much of it can be pleasurable, but eating too much can lead to obesity and disease. What seemed good at first — overeating — can very quickly show that it is bad in reality. The same is true of other sins, which sometimes can have an attractive veneer but which always have an ugly reality.

"In your dream, a Heavenly lady and I came to your rescue. I know reason well, and reason is important in recognizing what is good and bad. But more is needed than reason. The Heavenly lady represents divine guidance, which is something that is outside of reason. With reason and divine guidance, you can recognize sin and see how ugly it is in reality rather than be taken in by the attractive veneer it at first seems to have. Reason and divine guidance can and should work together.

"Please realize that the Siren is a liar. She said that she convinced Ulysses to stray from his path. That is not true. Ulysses' path went by the Siren. Ulysses was able to hear the song of the Siren and survive. He ordered his men to tie him to the mast of his ship so he could not jump overboard and swim to the Island of the Siren. His crewmen, however, put wax in their ears so that they could perform their duties without hearing the song of the Siren. Ulysses heard the song of the Siren, but he did not deviate from his path."

This is partially correct. Ulysses did not deviate from his literal path: His attempt to return to his home island of Ithaca continued. But his attempt to acquire knowledge of all things, bad and good, deviate from the path he ought to have taken: to acquire knowledge of what is good to know.

Virgil then said, "Let us continue climbing. Look upward. Paradise is calling to you."

A tame falcon will stay still until its master calls for it to soar. Now Dante strained to climb higher.

Dante and Virgil reached the fifth ledge of the mountain. There they saw saved souls, in tears, lying face down, their backs to the heavens and their faces looking at dust. Their hands and feet were bound.

Dante heard the souls say a prayer that was taken from Psalm 119 — "*Adhaesit Pavimento Anima Mea*" or "My Soul Cleaves Unto the Dust":

"My soul cleaves unto the dust: quicken You me according to Your word.

"I have declared my ways, and You heard me: teach me Your statutes.

"Make me to understand the way of Your precepts: so shall I talk of Your wondrous works.

"My soul melts for heaviness: strengthen You me according to Your word.

"Remove from me the way of lying: and grant me Your law graciously.

"I have chosen the way of truth: Your judgments have I laid before me.

"I have stuck unto Your testimonies: O Lord, put me not to shame.

"I will run the way of Your commandments, when You shall enlarge my heart."

Virgil said to the saved souls, "You will reach Paradise, and the purgation you are now undergoing is made easier by justice and the promise of Paradise. Please tell us how to reach the steps that lead upward."

A saved soul said, "If you are not required to spend time on this ledge purging your sin, go to the right, and you will find the steps that lead upward."

Dante thought, *This saved soul has mistaken Virgil and me for saved souls who do not need to spend time on this ledge. Some souls can skip ledges, if they are not guilty of the sin purged on that ledge. Also, it is good to note once more that the saved souls in Purgatory are helpful.*

Dante also thought, *I would like to talk to this saved soul.*

Virgil, who knew Dante's thoughts, nodded to him that it was OK to talk to the saved soul.

Dante said to the saved soul, "You are purifying yourself with tears, and you will see God. Please tell me who all of you were and why you weep in the dust. Also, can I help you in some way in the Land of the Living when I return?"

The saved soul replied, "I will tell you soon why we lie in the dust with our backs to Heaven, but first let me say that I was a successor to Saint Peter. In the Land of the Living, I was Pope Adrian V. I was Pope for only 38 days, but that was enough time for me to learn how difficult it is to be a good and virtuous Pope. I converted very late in life. When I became Pope, I understood how false the world is. I realized that true peace could not be found in this world. I instead sought the true peace that is found in Paradise.

"Until I came to the realization of the falseness of the world, I was greedy and I was separated from God. On this ledge we are punished for being greedy in life. Because we looked at money and material possessions in the Land of the Living instead of looking to God, on this ledge our purgation is to look at the dust of the ground and to turn our backs on God. Our hands and feet are bound because we used them to pursue money and material possessions with too much zeal in the Land of the Living. This is the worst punishment on the mountain."

Dante thought, *Each sinner is most horrified by his or own sin, and so each sinner regards his or her punishment as the worst because he or she must think constantly about that particular sin.*

This purgation is just because the avaricious turned their backs on Heaven, instead choosing to look toward money and material things. Now they are forced not to look toward Heaven. Because they used their hands and feet to pursue money and material things, now their hands and feet are tied.

Dante kneeled.

The saved soul said to him, "Why are you kneeling to me?"

Dante replied, "You have been a Pope. You have had high office."

The saved soul replied, "Please rise to your feet. Do not kneel to me. I am a servant, as are you and all the other souls here, of God. You know the words of Jesus when he was asked by the Pharisees which of seven husbands a woman had had in the Land of the Living would that woman be married to in Paradise: 'For when they shall rise from the dead, they neither marry, nor are given in marriage; but are as the angels who are in Heaven.'

"In the Land of the Living, I was married to my diocese, but now I am not married. The title of Pope is not applicable to one in the afterlife, and therefore you ought not to kneel to me.

"Please do not stay longer. Please let me go back to purging my sin. Let me cry in penance. In the Land of the Living, I have a niece named Alagia. I hope that she may retain her goodness and not be led astray. There is no lack of bad examples that she could follow. She is all that remains to me in the Land of the Living."

Dante thought, *The saved souls in Purgatory still care about and wish the best for people who are still in the Land of the Living. Also, on this ledge Virgil and I see the former Pope Adrian V being purged of the sin of greed. Of course, the Simoniac Popes in the Inferno were greedy, but they did not repent their sins before dying.*

Chapter 20: Fifth Ledge — Avarice and Wastefulness (Hugh Capet) (Purgatory)

Dante left then, respecting the wishes of Pope Adrian V. The desire to be purged of sin is more important than the desire to have a few more questions answered.

Virgil, as always, led the way. Many souls have been guilty of avarice, and this ledge was crowded. Walking along the outside of the ledge would have been dangerous, and so Virgil led Dante to the innermost part, next to the mountain. A narrow path was there.

Avarice is a sin that has captured many, many souls. Someday someone will come to drive away the She-Wolf that is avarice.

Dante and Virgil walked slowly, and Dante kept thinking about the souls lying face down on the ledge. From a soul ahead of Dante and Virgil came a voice crying out like a woman having the pain of giving birth, "Mary! Your poverty was shown by the place where you gave birth!"

Dante the Pilgrim thought, *I am beginning to piece together more information about the Mountain of Purgatory. On each ledge saved souls are given examples of a virtue they need to acquire and a sin they need to purge. So far, an event from the life of Mother Mary has been the first example of the virtue the saved souls need to acquire. That has been the case in the first five ledges of Purgatory Proper, and probably it will be the case with the two ledges Virgil and I still need to climb. The virtues that need to be acquired here are Charity and Detachment from Riches and What Riches can Buy, and the sin that needs to be purged is, of course, avarice, aka greed. The first example of the virtue that needs to be acquired is the Christmas story. Mary was pregnant and about to give birth, but no room was available in an inn; therefore, Mary gave birth in a stable and lay baby Jesus in a manger — a trough used to feed animals. She accepted this, and she did not complain about it.*

In Paradise, an angel thought, *If Mary had lived in a much later time, she may have given birth in a decrepit trailer park.*

The saved soul then cried out, "Good Fabricius, you chose to keep your virtue and be impoverished rather than to acquire vice and live in luxury."

Dante thought, *Gaius Fabricius Luscinus was incorruptible, refusing to take bribes, and he died without money to pay for his funeral or to provide dowries for his daughters. Fortunately, the Romans greatly respected him. The Romans paid for his burial, and the Romans paid for the dowries of his daughters. Fabricius valued virtue. He could have become rich by taking bribes when he served as Consul and as Censor, but he chose to stay poor.*

Dante was impressed by the words that the voice had spoken, and he pushed ahead to find out which saved soul the voice belonged to. As he did so, the voice spoke again, this time speaking of St. Nicholas, whom a later age would know as Santa Claus, and of the gold he had given to an impoverished father.

Dante thought, *Saint Nicholas provided dowries for three girls so that they could be married instead of being forced into prostitution. At that time and place, females needed a dowry in order to be married. Their father lacked the money to provide dowries for his three daughters and so it seemed that they would be forced to give up lives of virtue. Each night for three nights, Saint Nicholas threw a bag of gold through the window of the father's house, and the three bags of gold became the dowries for the father's three daughters.*

Dante said, "Saved soul, you who speak of such good things, please tell me who you are and why no one else is speaking. I can reward you with prayers when I return to the Land of the Living."

The saved soul replied, "I will help you, but not for any reward that I may win. I will help you because we souls in Purgatory are helpful, and because your presence here as a living man shows that God is showing you grace.

"I am Hugh Capet, and my descendants have been bad Kings of France. They have ruled from my time until the present day, and they have been named Louis and Philip.

"When the old line of Kings had died, my family was rich and influential enough to replace the old line. My descendants at first were not especially good, but they were not especially bad because they had a sense of shame.

"But then they became greedy. They annexed the kingdom of Provence to the kingdom of France, and then they annexed Ponthieu, Normandy, and Gascony.

"Let me tell you about three descendants of mine, all named Charles, and their sins, some that are already done and some that will be done. The first

Charles, of Anjou, defeated Manfred at the Battle of Benevento in 1266. He was so evil that people thought that he had poisoned Saint Thomas Aquinas and sent him to Paradise. Charles of Anjou thought that Saint Thomas was going to give a bad report about him to the 1274 Ecumenical Council of Lyons. Charles asked Saint Thomas what he was going to say about him. Saint Thomas replied, "Only the truth." People think that therefore Charles poisoned him.

"The second Charles is Charles of Valois, who serves Pope Boniface VIII. The Pope brought him to Italy to be a peacemaker, but his real job is to beat down the enemies of the Pope. This Charles, who is Philip the Fair's brother, will play a role in helping the Black Guelfs."

Dante thought, *I am a White Guelf, and I oppose the Black Guelfs.*

Hugh Capet thought, *This Charles will play a role in helping the Black Guelfs take over Florence. You, Dante, will be exiled.*

The saved soul continued, "The third Charles is Charles II, King of Naples. In return for a large amount of money, he will marry his young daughter to a much older man: Azzo VIII of Este. He will be like a pirate selling for as high a price as possible a female captive.

"These sins, past and future, are bad, but worst of all is a future sin. A Pope will be badly treated. A King of France — one of my descendants — will send troops to Anagni to take the Pope prisoner and treat him badly for three days, beating him and threatening to carry him off in chains and execute him. In doing this to a Pope, it is as if he is doing this to Christ Himself. Again Christ is mocked, and again Christ is crucified, and this Christ is crucified between two living thieves: the leaders of the forces this King of France sent against the Pope. I want to see this King of France punished. The Pope is the Vicar of Christ, and he ought not to endure such treatment."

Virgil thought, *I know the future. King Philip IV (aka the Fair) of France will send bullies to beat up Pope Boniface VIII, who will die on 11 October 1303, one month after he was badly beaten. Of course, Pope Boniface VIII will end up in the Inferno, but I know Dante well enough to know that he will find this bad treatment of a Pope — even a Pope who is his enemy — to be shocking. Dante would never approve of this kind of treatment for any Pope.*

The saved soul then said, "On this ledge, to purge avarice by day we saved souls cry aloud the examples of the virtues known as Charity and Detachment from Riches and What Riches can Buy and by night we cry aloud the examples of the sin known as avarice.

"By night we cry aloud the name Pygmalion. Dido was married to Sichaeus, but Pygmalion, her brother, killed him out of greed to steal Sichaeus' wealth. Because of that, Dido fled. Landing in northern Africa, she founded Carthage. In Virgil's *Aeneid*, she has an affair with Aeneas, and after he leaves her to fulfill his destiny in Italy, she commits suicide. She is in Circle 2 of the Inferno, which punishes the Lustful.

"By night we cry aloud the name Midas. He was so greedy that he wished that everything he touched would turn to gold. The god Bacchus heard and granted his prayer. Unfortunately, whenever Midas wanted to drink something, the liquid turned to gold. Whenever he tried to eat something, the food turned to gold. And when his young son ran to him for a hug, his son turned into a statue made of gold. Bacchus took back his gift when Midas requested him to.

"By night we cry aloud the name Achan. Joshua ordered the blowing of trumpets, and the walls of Jericho fell down, so the Jews conquered the city. The spoils of Joshua were supposed to be consecrated to, aka set aside for, the Lord, but a Jew named Achan stole some of the spoils: a good garment, and two hundred shekels of silver, and a wedge of gold of fifty shekels weight. He and his family were stoned to death — the other Jews threw heavy stones at them and killed them.

"By night we cry aloud the name Sapphira. Ananias and his wife, Sapphira, sold some land for the Apostles, but he kept part of the land (with his wife's knowledge) rather than selling all of the land and turning over all of the money to the Apostles. Peter rebuked him, and he fell dead. Later, Peter rebuked her, and she fell dead.

"By night we cry aloud the name Heliodorus. Heliodorus wanted to steal treasures from the temple in Jerusalem, but a man in golden armor appeared. The man was riding a horse that kicked Heliodorus. Also, two strong men whipped Heliodorus, and he was carried away in a litter.

"By night we cry aloud the name Polymnestor. Polymnestor was a King of Thrace to whom King Priam of Troy entrusted his son, Polydorus, in an attempt to keep him safe. Unfortunately, King Polymnestor coveted the treasure that the prince had, and out of greed, after Troy fell, he killed the prince so that he could steal the treasure.

"By night we cry aloud the name Crassus. Crassus is a very wealthy man from Roman history. He, Pompey, and Julius Caesar were triumvirs. Crassus led an army against the Parthians, who in 53 B.C.E. defeated him, cut off his head and right hand, and sent them to King Hyrodes. The King knew of Crassus' great wealth and of his greed for more wealth, and to mock the fallen enemy, he poured melted gold into the mouth of Crassus' head.

"By night we cry aloud these names. Sometimes, we cry these names loudly. Sometimes, we cry these names softly. By day we cry aloud the names of the virtuous you heard me crying. I am not the only one who cries these names. It was simply by chance that no other soul was crying the names of the virtuous when you heard me crying them."

Dante and Virgil had already started to continue their journey when the mountain shook as if an earthquake had struck. The island of Delos used to float freely until Jupiter rooted it so that it would be a stable place for his paramour Latona, aka Leto, to give birth to his twin children: the god Apollo and the goddess Diana. The mountain shook more than that moving island ever did.

All of the souls on the mountain cried out, and Virgil, afraid that Dante would be alarmed, said to him, "Don't worry. I am still here, and I am still your guide."

All the saved souls shouted, "*Gloria in excelsis Deo*." This song — "Glory to God in the Highest" — is the song that angels sang on the eve of the birth of Christ.

Dante and Virgil stood still and listened, just as the shepherds had listened to the angels. Then they walked on.

Dante wondered about the meaning of the shaking of the mountain and the shouting of the souls. He did not want to slow their pace by questioning Virgil, and so he walked on, wondering.

Chapter 21: Fifth Ledge — Avarice and Wastefulness (Purgatory)

Dante kept walking as he continued to wonder about the shaking of the mountain. He thirsted for the answers to his questions just as the woman of Samaria thirsted for the water of everlasting life that Jesus offered to her and to all. Dante also thought about the saved souls purging their sin on this ledge, and he grieved.

Suddenly a figure appeared just like the newly risen Christ had appeared to two apostles on the road to Emmaus. The figure appeared from behind Dante and Virgil as they carefully maneuvered through the saved souls who were lying on the ledge.

Dante and Virgil were not aware of the figure until he spoke to them: "May God give you peace, brothers."

Virgil greeted the figure and said, "I have appropriately been banished to Limbo by God, and I trust that God will appropriately lead you to Paradise."

The figure said, "I am surprised. If you two souls are appropriately banned from Paradise by God, how can it be that you are climbing this mountain?"

Dante thought, *We are on the shadowy side of the mountain. I am not casting a shadow, and so this figure does not know that I am still alive.*

Virgil said to the figure, "Look at the forehead of this man beside me. You will see the remaining Ps that the angel carved on his forehead. This man, who still lives, will eventually make his way to Paradise. But because he still lives and the Fates are still spinning his thread of life and the Fate named Athropos has not yet cut the thread, he cannot climb the mountain as we can. His eyes do not see as the eyes of souls do. Because he needed a guide, I was brought up from the Inferno to guide him, and I will do my duty and guide him as far as I can with the knowledge that I have.

"But can you tell me please why the mountain shook just now and why all the souls shouted, '*Gloria in excelsis Deo*,' as if with one voice?"

These were exactly the questions that Dante wanted to have answered, and he listened eagerly to the reply of the figure, who said, "This mountain is not subject to the natural laws that move the rest of this world. What causes earthquakes there does not cause earthquakes here. Heaven itself causes what happens here. In Purgatory Proper are no dew, no rain, no frost, no snow, no clouds, no lightning, no rainbows. An earthquake caused by natural laws can occur in Prepurgatory, but never in Purgatory Proper.

"Here in Purgatory Proper, the mountain shakes when a soul feels itself to have become purified. The mountain shakes with joy when a soul is purified enough to ascend to the top of the mountain and then to Paradise. And that is when all the saved souls shout with joy, '*Gloria in excelsis Deo*' or 'Glory to God in the highest.' The saved souls are not envious.

"The saved soul determines when its sins are purged and the saved soul is ready to climb to the top of the mountain. The saved soul is trustworthy. When it is not sufficiently purged of a particular sin, it desires to stay on the appropriate ledge and purge the sin. When that sin is sufficiently purged, it moves to a higher level. Not all souls need to spend time on each ledge. Some souls can skip a ledge and move to a higher ledge. It all depends on the kind of life that the soul lived while in a living body. When all sins are sufficiently purged, the soul moves to the top of the mountain and then to Paradise.

"Purging one's sins takes time. I have spent 500 years on this ledge, purging my sin of greed. I died in the year 96 C.E., and since this is the year 1300 C.E., I have been purging my sins for 1204 years. Only just now did I feel myself sufficiently purged of sin that I am ready to climb to the top of the mountain. This is why just now you felt the mountain shake and you heard souls shout. I hope that soon the other saved souls will be with God in Paradise."

Dante was happy. His thirst for knowledge had been quenched in a most satisfying way.

Virgil said to the figure, "Now I understand why the mountain shakes and the souls shout. You have broken through a net that bound you. Please tell me who you are, and why you have lain on this ledge for 500 years."

The figure replied, "I was alive during the reign of the Roman Emperor Titus, who, with justice and before he became Emperor, revenged the crucifixion of Christ by destroying Jerusalem and defeating the Jews in 70 C.E.

"I was a pagan, but I became a Christian.

"I was a poet — a title that long endures and is much honored. I was, others say, a major poet of Rome's Silver Age. I wrote the *Thebaid*, which told of the Seven Against Thebes. Oedipus ruled Thebes, and after he died, his two sons, Eteocles and Polynices, decided to take turns ruling the city. Eteocles would rule for a year, and then Polynices would rule for a year, and so they would alternate as rulers of Thebes. However, after Eteocles' first year of rule, he was greedy and refused to let Polynices rule for the following year. Polynices raised an army. Thebes had seven gates, and the seven captains in the army raised by Polynices each attacked one of the seven gates. The two brothers fought in single combat, and they killed each other.

"I also started to write the *Achilleid*, an epic poem about Achilles, the greatest warrior of the Trojan War, but I died before I could complete it.

"My name is Statius, and I am still famous in the Land of the Living.

"I became a poet because of Virgil's *Aeneid*, the epic poem that also caused more than 999 other people to become poets. The *Aeneid* is the mother of my poetry and of much other poetry. I learned how to write poetry from the *Aeneid*; without that model, my poetry would have been worthless. I wish I had been alive when Virgil was alive. I would willingly spend another year on this ledge if only that would happen."

Virgil looked at Dante and silently communicated, *Don't tell him who I am.*

But Dante had already started smiling, anticipating Statius' joy when he found out that Virgil was standing before him. He quickly stopped smiling, but too late — Statius had already seen the smile.

Statius looked at Dante and requested, "Please tell me why you were smiling just now. You quickly smiled and quickly stopped smiling."

Dante was standing between two souls. One soul wanted him to tell what he knew, and the other soul did not want him to tell what he knew.

Dante sighed, and Virgil relented and said to him, "Feel free to tell this soul what he wants to know."

Dante said to Statius. "I was smiling because my guide who is helping me climb to Paradise is Virgil, the one who taught you how to write poetry that sings the deeds of gods and of men."

Statius was happy and was kneeling so he could hug Virgil's knees to show him respect, but Virgil said to him, "Don't. You are a saved soul, and I am not. You should not show me reverence."

Statius relented, stood up, and said, "Now you can understand how much I respect you and your poetry."

Dante thought, *Purgatory has surprises, and the surprises are good surprises. Statius said that he would love to meet Virgil, and here Virgil is.*

The three poets walked on: Virgil, a pagan who had stayed a pagan; Statius, a pagan who had become a Christian; and Dante, a Christian.

Chapter 22: Sixth Ledge — Gluttony (Statius) (Purgatory)

Dante and Virgil and Statius had passed the angel, who had removed another P from the foreheads of Dante and Statius, and the three poets had begun climbing to the next ledge. The angel had said, "Blessed are they who thirst after righteousness," leaving out the words "hunger and."

Dante, now feeling lighter than he had at any time since he had started climbing up the mountain, easily followed Virgil and Statius.

Virgil said to Statius, "Love always kindles love, if the first love is virtuous and is clearly seen. You showed much love to me when you tried to kneel and embrace my knees, as was the custom of our times. Now let me tell you that when Juvenal, who lived at the same time as you, first entered Limbo, he told me of the great love you bore me. Since then, I have felt for you as much love as it is possible to feel for a person I had never seen. Our journey will now seem much shorter because we can enjoy each other's company.

"But please tell me, if you will, how can it be that you were greedy? You have acquired much good sense, as can be seen from the diligence with which you educated yourself to write poetry."

Statius smiled briefly, and then he said, "Your words show that you must really love me. Appearances can be misleading. Because you found me on this ledge and because all the sinners whom you have seen so far have apparently been guilty of greed, you assume that my sin was greed. Actually, I was far from greedy — too far! My sin, which I have been purging for thousands of months, was the opposite of greed: prodigality. Instead of valuing money too much, I valued the things that money can buy too much, and I spent all I had, and more.

"Extremes are evil. I should have learned from Aristotle's mean between extremes earlier in my life. Keeping in mind Aristotle's Golden Mean, we can understand that both extremes (too much and too little) are sins. When it comes to handling money, it is wrong to save every penny you make and never spend money on necessities, and it is wrong to spend every penny you make and every penny you can borrow on things that you don't need. I was guilty of overspending.

"I learned to repent my sin from some lines that you, Virgil, wrote: "Accursed love for gold / To what extremes will you drive us?" You wrote about greed, but because I had studied Aristotle's Golden Mean, I began to think about the opposite extreme, and so I realized that I had sinned, and I repented. If not for your lines, I would be in the Inferno. Instead, I repented that sin, and all of my other sins.

"In the Inferno, the avaricious and the prodigal are in the same place, but they are in conflict, slamming huge boulders against each other. Here in Purgatory we have cooperation rather than conflict, as the avaricious and the prodigal work together to purge their sins. But here in Purgatory, as in the Inferno, sinners who engaged in opposites can be found together.

"On Judgment Day, many will rise not knowing that prodigality is a vice, and not having repented that sin.

"I repented that sin, and I became a Christian, and so I have spent 500 years on this ledge among the greedy purging my sin of prodigality."

Virgil said to Statius, "When you wrote the *Thebaid*, you gave no indication that you were a Christian. If it is true that you were not a Christian then, what caused you to become a Christian later?"

Statius replied, "Again, it was some verses that you had written that directed me to Christianity. First, you influenced me to become a poet and then you, although you were not a Christian, influenced me to become a Christian. You were like a traveler who holds a lantern behind him. The light does not help the traveler to see, but it does help the people behind him to see.

"Virgil, you wrote, 'A new age is dawning, / Justice is returning, and the first age of Humankind, / And a new child comes from Heaven.'

"Christianity had arisen in the Roman Empire, and I listened to Christians, and what they said matched what you had prophesied. When the Roman Emperor Domitian persecuted the Christians, I wept as they suffered. During my lifetime, I helped the Christians. I also learned that theirs was the true faith. Before I had written the seventh book of the *Thebaid*, I had been baptized. But out of fear of the persecutions of Emperor Diocletian, I kept my Christianity secret. For many years, I pretended to be a pagan, and because of my lack of zeal I spent 400 years running with the slothful on the fourth ledge.

"Now, Virgil, please tell me, where is Terence, the Roman comic playwright?

"Where is Plautus, the Roman comic playwright?

"Where is Caecilius, the Roman comic playwright?

"Where is Varius, the Roman writer of tragedies and epics?

"All of these poets died before Jesus Christ appeared on earth. Are they in the Inferno? If so, in which circle are they?"

Virgil replied, "All of them, along with Persius, the Roman satirist, are with me, and with the Greek epic poet Homer, whom the Muses blessed more than any other poet, in Limbo, the first circle of the Inferno. We often talk about Parnassus, the mountain of the nine Muses. Also with us are the Greek tragedian Euripides, the Greek tragic poet Antiphon, the Greek lyric poet Simonides, and the Greek tragic poet Agathon.

"Also in Limbo are many people whom you wrote about: Antigone and Ismene, who are the daughters of Oedipus and Jocasta; Argia, the wife of Polynices; Hypsipyle, who conducted Kings such as Adrastus to a fountain when they needed water; and King Lycomedes' daughter Deidamia, one of the young women among whom Achilles was hidden after his mother, Thetis, disguised him as a young woman."

They had reached the ledge. They were silent as they stood on the ledge. The time was between 10 and 11 a.m., and Virgil said, "Let's walk toward the right."

Statius agreed, and they started walking. Dante listened closely as Virgil and Statius talked about poetry.

Soon, they came to a tree that had fruit with a pleasant odor. The tree resembled an upside-down fir tree. Its branches grew wider toward the top, preventing any souls from climbing the tree. A stream of water also fell onto the tree.

Virgil and Statius drew closer to the tree, and a voice shouted, "You cannot eat this fruit, and you cannot drink this water."

Then the voice coming from the tree shouted examples of temperance, the virtue that is opposed to gluttony:

"Mary was worried because the wine ran out at the wedding feast in Cana. Mary did not care about the wine for the alcohol's sake, but she did care about the marriage being celebrated properly. She persuaded her son, Jesus, to perform his first miracle, turning water into wine.

"The ancient Roman women did not feel the need to drink wine; instead, they drank water.

"Because Daniel would not eat the food of King Nebuchadnezzar or drink the drink of the King, he was given prophetic powers.

"In Humankind's earliest history, acorns served well as food and water served well as drink.

"John the Baptist lived in the desert, where he ate locusts and wild honey. John the Baptist prophesied the coming of the Messiah."

Chapter 23: Sixth Ledge — Gluttony (Forese Donati) (Purgatory)

Dante looked up at the tree, trying to see from where the voice was coming.

Virgil called to him, "Dante, we need to make better use of our time. Let's go."

Dante quickly turned and followed Virgil and Statius and listened — with profit — to their conversation. Suddenly, the three poets heard chanting: "You shall open my lips, O Lord: and my mouth shall show Your praise."

Dante asked Virgil, "What am I hearing?"

Virgil replied, "Most likely, the voices are coming from saved souls who are purging their sin and therefore paying off their debt to God."

A group of souls, now silent, came up behind them. These penitents had been gluttons. While alive, they should have used their mouths to praise God instead of eating and drinking too much. Like monks, they now sometimes sang and sometimes were silent. The souls noticed Dante's shadow, looked at him doubtfully, and then — their eyes still on the prize — walked past him and the other two poets.

These saved souls were emaciated. Their eyes were sunken and surrounded by dark shadows. Their bones could be seen clearly.

Dante thought, *These souls remind me of Erysichthon, who cut down trees that were sacred to the goddess Ceres. He himself cut down a tree that was hung with wreaths: one wreath for each prayer that Ceres had granted. By cutting down the sacred tree, he killed a dryad nymph: the deity of the tree. In revenge, the nymph cursed him. Ceres heard the curse and punished Erysichthon by making him endlessly hungry. The more he ate, the hungrier he became. He sold all of his possessions to buy food to consume. He even sold his own daughter for money to buy food and eventually cannibalized his own flesh.*

These souls also remind me of Miriam. During the siege of Jerusalem in A.D. 70, Miriam, according to the Jewish historian Josephus, was so hungry that she cooked and ate her own baby boy. She acted like a bird of prey cannibalizing its own young.

Dante the Poet remembered, *The eye sockets of the penitents were clearly visible. Anyone looking at the penitents' faces would have clearly seen the letters*

O and M and O in their faces: The two O's are the eye sockets, and the M is the middle of the face (eyebrows and nose). The word 'omo' — or 'homo' — is Latin for man, and believers say that when God made Humankind, He put his mark on each human being.

Who would think — without knowing the nature of souls and how Purgatory works — that these souls who smell the fruit of the tree and who smell the stream of water that falls on the tree could be so emaciated?

Suddenly, one of the shades turned toward Dante and said, "This is a blessing that I have received from God!"

Dante recognized this soul from his voice; the soul was so emaciated that Dante could not recognize him from his face and body. This soul was his friend Forese Donati.

Dante thought, *We used to write comic insult poems about each other and send them to each other. I criticized Forese for his gluttony and his huge belly. He wrote that I was once so afraid that I filled my pants with a substance that polite people don't mention except when talking to their physician.*

Forese said to him, "Ignore the way I look: the sickly skin and shriveled flesh. Tell me about yourself and the two souls with you. Who are they? Please tell me your story!"

Dante replied, "When you died, I wept. And now I feel like weeping again seeing you as emaciated as you are. What has stripped the flesh from your body? Don't ask me to speak. I am in shock at how you look, and I cannot talk well in such a state."

Forese replied, "The tree with its fruit and with a stream falling onto it makes me lean. God has given the tree that power. All of us here fill our mouths with words to repent our sin of gluttony rather than fill our mouths with food and drink to make our bellies bigger. The tree makes us hungry and emaciated, and each time we go around this ledge our hunger and emaciation are increased. People may call this pain, but it is also solace. On the cross, Christ called out, "My God, my God, why have You forsaken me?" Christ did not want to be on the cross, but He did what had to be done to redeem Humankind. He was eager to help Humankind. We are eager to do what has to be done to purge our sin of gluttony."

Dante said, "Forese, you died not even five years ago. You repented late in life, so how were you able to climb so high up this mountain so quickly? I thought that I would see you in Prepurgatory with the late repentant."

Forese said, "I had a good wife who has been a good widow. Nella cried for me, and she has prayed for me. Only because of her prayers, which come from a virtuous person, have I been able to climb so high and so quickly up this mountain. Because of her, I have been able to skip the other ledges.

"Both God and I love Nella, and she stands out in contrast with other women who lack her virtue. In Sardinia are wild women who go about with bare breasts. These wild women have more virtue than the women who are my Nella's neighbors in Florence. Those 'ladies' of Florence go about with too-low necklines. Muslims dress much more modestly by their own choice. Trouble is coming to Florence, and if the 'ladies' of Florence knew the trouble that awaits them, they would scream. They will experience much trouble before the infants they now are holding grow up and grow beards.

"But now, Dante, tell me your story. I and my fellow penitents are looking at your shadow and are wondering how a living man has come to climb this mountain."

Dante replied, "When you think about some of the times we spent together in the Land of the Living, you must cringe from some of the sins we committed. Because of my sins, my guide came to me to be my leader a few days ago. We journeyed through the Inferno, and then my guide led me up this mountain. He will be my guide until I meet Beatrice, whom you knew, and then Beatrice will take over as my guide.

"The other soul with me is that soul for whom the mountain trembled recently, showing that he is ready to enter Paradise."

Chapter 24: Sixth Ledge — Gluttony (Bonagiunta da Lucca) (Purgatory)

The conversation of Dante and Forese Donati did not slow down their journey. They walked as they talked, and their speed was like that of a ship with favorable winds.

The saved souls marveled at Dante because they knew that he cast a shadow and was a living man.

Continuing to answer Forese's question about the souls who were traveling with him, Dante said, "And this second soul could travel much faster up the mountain, but he is acting courteously as a companion to us.

"But please, tell me, where is the soul of Piccarda, your sister? Also, among these souls, is there anyone I should know?"

Forese answered Dante's first question: "Piccarda, my sister, is already enjoying Paradise. She was both virtuous and beautiful."

Then he answered Dante's second question: "I can name the souls here — no reason not to."

Dante thought, *In the Inferno, souls in the lower circles did not want to be named. They did not want their names — and deeds! — to be remembered in the Land of the Living. Here in Purgatory, souls do not mind being named.*

Forese pointed out several souls and named them: "Here is Bonagiunta Orbicciani of Lucca, a poet who was fond of drinking wine.

"Here is Pope Martin IV, who too much enjoyed eating too much of his meals of Lake Bolsena eels, which he ordered to be stewed in wine.

"Here is Ubaldino della Pila, a great entertainer and a great feaster. His son is in the Inferno. You may have seen him as you journeyed through Hell: he is the Archbishop Ruggieri, and Ugolino is gnawing his scalp. Another of his relatives is entombed with Farinata in the circle of the heretics. Ubaldino once played host — for months — to the Pope and entertained and fed him and his entourage lavishly."

Dante thought, *Your family does not determine where you end up in the afterlife. The same family can have damned souls and saved souls.*

Forese continued, "Here is Boniface de' Fieschi of Genova, a wealthy Archbishop of Ravenna who fed his entourage feasts but neglected to feed the multitudes spiritual food."

Dante thought, *Both Ubaldino della Pila and Boniface de' Fieschi of Genova are so hungry that I see them before me trying to bite the air.*

Forese finished, "Here is Milord Marchese, a member of the Argogliosi family. When people complained that he did nothing but drink wine, he said that he was always thirsty. Now he is thirstier."

Dante looked around. One soul in particular seemed to want to speak to him: Bonagiunta Orbicciani of Lucca. Dante thought that he heard him say softly the name of a woman: "Gentucca."

Dante said to Bonagiunta, "Soul, you seem to want to speak to me. Please speak so that I may better hear you."

Bonagiunta said, "Let me prophesy to you. A woman has been born who, still not yet married, will soon give care to you and cause you to praise the city I was from in the Land of the Living, although that city is now reviled. Remember this prophecy. If it is not clear now, it will be clear later when it occurs."

Virgil thought, *This is a prophecy of Dante's upcoming exile from Florence, about which other souls will tell him more clearly later and which he will experience soon.*

Bonagiunta continued, "But aren't you the poet who wrote a poem in the new style, a poem that began, "Ladies who have knowledge of love"?

Virgil thought, *Lots of poets are present now. We wrote in various languages. I wrote in Latin, but these poets wrote in vernacular Italian. In addition, we wrote various kinds of poetry in various styles. I wrote epic poetry, Forese wrote comic poetic insults, and other poets, including Dante, wrote love poetry. In addition, Dante wrote in a sweet new style in which Bonagiunta did not write. Dante has something to learn here, or he would not be on this ledge having this conversation with this particular poet.*

Statius read me, and he learned something from me that I did not know was in my own work. Statius learned enough from me that he was able to decide to become a Christian. Perhaps Dante will be able to learn something from these vernacular poets who wrote love poetry. Perhaps, like Statius did from me, Dante will be able to learn from these vernacular poets something about Christianity as well as about poetry.

The poem Bonagiunta mentioned is a different poem from the poem that Casella attempted to sing in Prepurgatory. That poem was a silly love song. The poem Bonagiunta mentioned marks an important shift not just in style, but in content. In this newer poem, Dante says that he realizes that his happiness lies not in love games but in praising Beatrice. This is a different, more spiritual kind of love.

Not all kinds of love are good. Remember Francesca da Rimini in the Inferno? Passionate and adulterous love got her an eternal residence in the Inferno. She blamed her problems on lots of things, including a book about an adulterous love affair between Queen Guinever and Sir Lancelot. Some kinds of love and some kinds of writing about love can be bad.

When Dante returns to the Land of the Living, he must be careful to write about love carefully and accurately. Perhaps Dante needs to Christianize the love he writes about. Statius was able to read me and Christianize my Fourth Eclogue. Perhaps Dante needs to Christianize his love poetry when he writes new poetry after he returns to the Land of the Living.

Dante replied to Bonagiunta, "I am a poet who, when Love inspires me, pays attention and writes down what I have learned."

Dante thought, *This is true. I have learned and advanced as a poet. The poem that Casella wanted to sing in Prepurgatory is much earlier and much worse than the poem that Bonagiunta just mentioned. The poem that Casella wanted to sing appeared in* Convivio, *an early work of mine. The poem that Bonagiunta mentioned just now appeared in* Vita Nuova, *a more recent work of mine. Maybe when I return to the Land of the Living, I can write an even better work. Maybe I can write about the love of God, both the love He has for us and the love that good people have for Him.*

Bonagiunta said, "Now I see what I was missing when I wrote poetry. My poetry never reached the high level that your poetry has achieved. My lack of paying close attention to Love held me back, and it held back poets like me. If I had continued learning, I could have written better about Love and I could have written better poetry."

The emaciated saved souls, except for Forese, left Dante, Virgil, and Statius, seeming to take off like birds.

Forese was like a runner who, tired, slowed down and let the other runners pass him. Forese asked Dante, "When will we meet again?"

Dante replied, "When I return to the Land of the Living, I do not know how long I shall stay there. Even if I die soon thereafter, my heart will already have reached this island because Florence loses virtue each day and is ruining itself."

Forese said, "Here is one good thing that will happen soon. The worst citizen of Florence will end up in the Inferno. The justice that is in Paradise will make itself known. If you do not understand me now, you will later."

Virgil thought, *This is a prophecy about Forese's brother, Corso Donati. He is the leader of the Black Guelfs in Florence, and he will persuade Pope Boniface VIII to send Charles of Valois to Florence to kick out the White Guelfs. Corso will be responsible for Dante's upcoming exile. Corso was also cruel to Piccarda, his sister. She entered a nunnery to serve God, but he forced her to leave the nunnery and marry someone who would help Corso achieve his political goals. Corso will attempt to gain complete control over Florence, but the Black Guelfs will stop him and condemn him to death. Corso will attempt to escape, but the Black Guelfs will kill him during the escape attempt.*

One's family does not determine where one ends up in the afterlife. Of the Donati family, Piccarda is in Paradise, Forese is climbing the Mountain of Purgatory, and Corso will end up in the Inferno.

Forese continued, "Now it is time for me to leave you. We have spoken a long time, and time is precious to souls who are purging their sins."

Forese then quickly left, running after the other emaciated saved souls.

Dante walked with Virgil and Statius. Before them soon appeared another tree that had fruit. The emaciated saved souls were under the tree, arms reaching high, asking for fruit, but being denied. Eventually, the souls gave up and continued their journey on the ledge.

The three poets came close to the tree, and a voice came from among its leaves, saying, "Don't stop walking. Don't come close. At the top of the mountain is a tree, and the tree you see here is an offshoot of that higher tree."

Dante, Virgil, and Statius stayed close to the cliff and passed the tree.

As they passed the tree, the voice called out examples of gluttony: "At the wedding of Pirithous and Hippodamia, the Centaurs got drunk and tried to rape the bride and other women at the wedding. Theseus and the Lapithae defended the women and killed many Centaurs.

"Gideon had many soldiers. When they arrived at a river, they were very thirsty. Gideon, following the advice of God, watched his soldiers. Some put their faces in the water and drank greedily. This was a mistake because they were not on the lookout for danger. Other, more cautious, soldiers cupped the water in their hands and brought the water up to their faces, thus remaining vigilant. Gideon led these vigilant soldiers to victory."

The three poets continued walking, and suddenly heard a voice: "You three who are alone, what are you thinking?"

The voice came from a fiery-red angel who had noticed that three figures were walking together in a place where saved souls gathered in much larger groups.

The angel said to them, "If you are looking for the way up, here it is. This is the path used by those who seek peace."

The brilliance of the angel blinded Dante. By using the sense of sound, he followed Virgil and Statius.

The angel touched Dante's forehead and erased another of the P's, leaving just one remaining. Dante smelled something sweet, and he heard these words that were spoken by the angel: "Blessed are they who hunger after righteousness instead of after excessive amounts of food."

Chapter 25: Seventh Ledge — Lust (Body-Soul Relationship) (Purgatory)

The time was around 2 p.m., and the three poets started climbing the stairs to the next ledge: the ninth of nine ledges. They walked in single file because of the narrowness of the stairs, and they did not waste time.

Dante wanted to speak. He wanted to ask a question that had been occupying his mind for a long time: ever since he had seen the emaciated saved souls of ledge six. He began to speak, changed his mind, and was silent.

Virgil, however, as always, knew his thoughts, and encouraged Dante to speak.

Dante asked, "Why are the saved souls on ledge six so emaciated? These souls are purging the sin of gluttony, but why are they so emaciated? After all, souls do not need food and drink."

Virgil said, "Think of two analogies, and they will help you to understand the answer to your questions.

"First think of the myth of Meleager. When he was born, his mother learned from the Fates that Meleager would live only as long as a piece of wood that was then burning in the fireplace would remain unburned. His mother, Althaea, grabbed the piece of wood, put the fire out, and put the piece of wood in a safe place. Meleager grew up and became a warrior and a hero. When the goddess Diana sent a boar to ravage Calydon, Meleager led a band of heroes to hunt the dangerous boar. Eventually, he was able to kill it. He presented the hide to Atalanta, with whom he was in love, but his uncles — his mother's brothers — stole the hide from her. Outraged, Meleager killed his uncles. When his mother learned of her brothers' deaths, she put the half-burned piece of wood in a fire, and Meleager died as the piece of wood burned. In this myth, two things — Meleager and a piece of wood — are very different but are closely related, and when something happens to the first of the pair, it affects the second of the pair.

"In addition, think of a mirror. It reflects every movement of the person in front of it. The mirror and the person are very different, but one thing imitates perfectly every movement of the other thing.

"But Statius can answer your question in more detail."

Statius said to Virgil, "As you request, I will explain to him things he does not know. I have too much respect for you to deny your request."

Then Statius said to Dante, "As you know, the year is 1300. Science has barely made a beginning, and some of what you 'know' is incorrect. As I am in the afterlife, I can see ahead into at least part of the future, and I know that science will make great increases in what Humankind knows. Science will be one of the greatest accomplishments of Humankind.

"Let me explain some things to you, using a little science but also using religion. Each can reveal truth. I will explain to you how a baby acquires a soul, and I will explain to you the aerial body: the body you see when you look at me or Virgil or any soul.

"Conception may occur after a human male deposits semen into the womb of a human woman who is ready to have a baby. Assume that it does occur. The first part of the soul becomes present. We can call this the vegetative part: it takes nourishment and it grows. The fetus grows, and it begins to move. The second part of the soul becomes present. We can call this the sensitive part: it uses its senses such as the sense of touch and it moves. At the time of quickening, when the fetus can be felt moving in the womb, God breathes the third part of the soul into the fetus. We can call this the intellective part: it can contemplate itself and it can think. With this third part present, the soul is complete. The Spanish philosopher Averroës erred by denying the third part of the soul, which gives it immortality.

"When the body dies, the soul is freed, and it goes either to the Inferno or to the Mountain of Purgatory. The soul retains memory, intelligence, and will, but it lacks its vegetative and sensitive parts until it acquires its aerial body, which is formed from the air around it. This aerial body is visible, and it is often called a 'shade.' This aerial body can move and it has all five senses. The aerial body can speak, and it can laugh, and it can cry, and it can sigh. The aerial body also reflects the feelings of the soul: it changes with those feelings. Thus, if the soul is hungry, the aerial body can take on the appearance of emaciation. This should answer your question. My words also explain how you are able to see the souls you have seen in the Inferno and on the Mountain of Purgatory.

"Let me summarize a few main points of Christian doctrine:

"First, God directly creates the human soul.

"Second, each body is given a soul.

"Third, body and soul, joined, become one unified person.

"Fourth, even after the death of the body, the soul continues to exist."

The three poets continued walking and reached the next ledge. Then they saw a fire. Only a narrow space along the edge of the ledge was without fire. The three poets had to walk in that space in single file.

Dante was terrified by the narrowness of the path left to walk on. On one side was the fire; on the other side was air and no solid ground to walk on.

Virgil told Dante, "Be sure to walk on the narrow path. This is a place where it is easy to make a misstep."

Then the three poets heard a song — "*Summae Deus Clementiae*" or "God of Supreme Clemency" — that asked God to banish lustful thoughts and to cleanse the sinner with healing fire:

"Great God of boundless mercy hear;

"You Ruler of this earthly sphere;

"In substance one, in Persons three,

"Dread Trinity in Unity!

"Do You in love accept our lays

"Of mingled penitence and praise;

"And set our hearts from error free,

"More fully to rejoice in You.

"Our reins and hearts in pity heal,

"And with Your chastening fire anneal;

"Gird You our loins, each passion quell,

"And every harmful lust expel.

"Now as our anthems, upward borne,

"Awake the silence of the morn,

"Enrich us with Your gifts of grace,

"From Heaven, Your blissful dwelling place!

"Hear You our prayer, Almighty King;

"Hear You our praises, while we sing,

"Adoring with the Heavenly host

"The Father, Son, and Holy Ghost."

The song was coming from the fire. Dante looked and saw souls walking in the fire. He made sure that he stayed on the narrow path.

When the souls had sung the entire hymn, they shouted, *"Virum non cognosco."*

Dante thought, *This is an example of the virtue of Chastity. As always on the Mountain of Purgatory, the first example of a virtue comes from the life of Mary. When the angel told Mary that she would give birth to the Savior, she replied, "Virum non cognosco" or in English "I know not man." In other words, she was a virgin. Of course, she did as God willed and although she was a virgin, she gave birth.*

The souls in the fire sang the hymn again, and then they called, "Diana banished Helice."

Dante thought, *Diana is the Roman name of the Greek goddess Artemis, who was one of the three virgin Greek goddesses. The other virgin goddesses are Minerva and Vesta. Diana was a militant virgin. When Jupiter seduced one of her attendants, the nymph Helice, Diana dismissed her. Helice gave birth to Arcas. Juno was Jupiter's jealous wife. She turned Helice into a she-bear, and Jupiter placed her into a constellation: Ursa Major. "Ursa Major" means "Big Bear" or "Great Bear."*

Again, the souls sang the hymn, and then they praised virtuous husbands and wives.

Dante thought, *These couples refrained from having coercive sex. In addition, they refrained from having affairs. These couples are not virgins. Certainly, married couples are allowed to have sex with each other. It is a heresy to believe that proper sex is sinful. Used properly, sex is far from sinful and is one of the great pleasures of life. After all, God invented sex.*

Chapter 26: Seventh Ledge — Lust (Guido Guinizelli and Arnaut Daniel) (Purgatory)

The three poets continued walking, and Dante cast a shadow that touched the flame and changed its color, making it a deeper red.

The souls inside the flame noticed this and marveled, "His body seems to be made of flesh and blood!"

Some souls came close to Dante, but they were careful to stay within the fire and continue the purgation of their sin.

A soul said to Dante, "You who bring up the rear out of respect for the two souls ahead of you, please tell us how you are able to cast a shadow as if you had avoided death. All of us within the fire would like to know."

Dante was about to answer, but he saw another group of souls approaching this group of souls — the two groups were walking in opposite directions on the ledge. One group walked the ledge clockwise; the other group walked the ledge counterclockwise.

The two groups of souls exchanged a brief, chaste kiss that reminded Dante that St. Paul wrote in Romans 16:16, "Salute one another with a holy kiss."

The two groups of souls did not linger; they kissed and kept moving, intent on purging their sin.

Both groups shouted. The group that had just arrived shouted, "Sodom, Gomorrah."

Dante thought, *I can guess that this group of souls consists of people who misused homosexual sex in some way. Sodom and Gomorrah were cities that contained homosexuals, and in these cities homosexual rape — a clear misuse of sex — occurred. In Genesis 19:1-11, we read that two angels, who resembled human men, visited Lot in Sodom. That night, men of Sodom came to Lot's house and ordered him to give them the two men who were visiting him so that they could "know" the two men. "Know" is used here in the Biblical sense: to have sex with. In addition, the men of Sodom didn't care about getting consent before having sexual intercourse. In other words, when the Sodomites say, "Bring them out to us so that we may know them," they are really saying, "Bring them out to us so that we may homosexually rape them." Of course, the angels are not raped. When the men of Sodom attempt to rape the angels, the angels blind them. This story concerns homosexual rape.*

Other non-Biblical stories about Sodom and Gomorrah exist. The inhabitants of both Sodom and Gomorrah were suspicious of strangers. Anyone who was different from them in any way they treated badly. Strangers in Sodom and Gomorrah were placed on a bed. If they were too long to fit in the bed, their legs were chopped off so they would fit. If they weren't long enough to fit in the bed, they were placed on a rack and stretched until they fit the bed. And so the inhabitants of Sodom and Gomorrah forced anyone who was different from them to conform.

In addition, the inhabitants of Sodom and Gomorrah were said to not allow beggars into the city. But when they did allow a beggar into the city, they would each give the beggar a coin. The beggar would be happy to get the coins because he thought that he could buy food with it. However, each coin had the name of an inhabitant of the city written on it. The sellers of food would look at the coins, see the names, and would not sell the beggar food. Also, the beggar was not allowed to leave the city. When the beggar starved to death, the inhabitants of the city would stop by the corpse and take back their coins.

The inhabitants of Sodom and Gomorrah did not love their neighbor and did not treat other people the way that the inhabitants of Sodom and Gomorrah wanted to be treated.

The other group of souls shouted, "Pasiphaë and the bull."

Dante thought, *I can guess that this group of souls consists of heterosexuals. Pasiphaë was guilty of misusing sex. In particular, she was guilty of bestiality: having sex with an animal. She was a Queen of Crete who fell in love with a bull, so she commissioned Daedalus to create an artificial cow for her to creep into. The bull made love to the artificial cow (and to Pasiphaë), and Pasiphaë conceived and gave birth to the Minotaur, a mythical half-human, half-bull creature that feasted on human flesh. This story relates to an abuse of heterosexual sex, although it concerns a form of sodomy, which includes sex between human beings and animals. The heterosexual sinners acted like animals, giving in to lust instead of using human reason to control lust, and the Pasiphaë myth is an extreme form of acting like an animal.*

After kissing, the two groups separated and continued walking, crying tears of mourning because of the sins that they had committed.

Dante then answered the question that the souls had asked him, saying, "You souls are destined for Paradise. Please know that my body and soul have not been separated. My body is here, walking beside you. My body has flesh, blood, and bones. I am climbing the Mountain of Purgatory because in my life I have been blind. A lady who resides in Paradise has won for me a great gift. In order that my eyes be opened, I am now allowed to walk while still alive through your world.

"Please, tell me who you are. Who is in this group? And who is in the group of saved souls who walk in the opposite direction? I will make known in the Land of the Living your answers to my questions."

The souls were surprised at who Dante — still a living man — was, but the soul who had earlier spoken to Dante said, "From the experience you are having now, you can die a better death than you would have suffered otherwise.

"The shades who move in the opposite direction to ours were guilty of the same sin that got Caesar called 'Queen' as he rode in triumph."

Dante thought, *When he was a young man, Julius Caesar was an ambassador to the court of King Nicomedes IV of Bithynia. Caesar supposedly had a homosexual relationship with the King, something that led to his political enemies calling him the Queen of Bithynia. As I thought, the other group of souls consists of homosexuals.*

The soul continued, "Therefore, that group of souls shouts 'Sodom' as they walk around the ledge.

"The sin of my group of souls is the misuse of heterosexual sex. We did not act like human beings and use our reason so we could do the right thing; instead, we gave in to our lust and acted like animals. That is why we shout 'Pasiphaë' as we walk around the ledge."

"Now you know our guilt. If you want to know our names, too many souls are here for me to name, and anyway, I don't know everyone's name.

"My name is Guido Guinizelli. I died in 1276, and I climbed so high up the mountain in only 24 years because I repented my sins early in life."

Dante thought, *I know the poetry of Guido Guinizelli. He was a forerunner of those of us who write in the sweet new style. He is a poet of genius.*

Dante told him that he would be happy to help him in any way possible, and the poet said, "I am happy to hear that, but please tell why you are willing to help me in any way possible?"

Dante replied, "I have read, studied, and learned your poetry, which is and will be valuable as long as poetry is known."

Guinizelli pointed to a soul and said, "This man is a poet who wrote in his native language better than I wrote in mine. Some people do not value him enough. They think that other poets are better, but they base their opinion on reputations, not on the actual poetry itself.

"But please say a *Paternoster* for me when you climb to Paradise — at least the part that applies to me."

Dante thought, *The* Paternoster *is the Lord's Prayer: "Our Father who is in Heaven, holy be Your name. Your kingdom come, Your will be done, on Earth as it is in Heaven. Give us this day our daily bread. And forgive us our debts, as we forgive our debtors. And lead us not into temptation, but deliver us from evil. For Yours is the kingdom, and the power, and the glory, for ever. Amen." The part that does not apply to Guinizelli or any other of the saved souls on the Mountain of Purgatory is "lead us not into temptation."*

Guinizelli then left to make room for another soul. He vanished into the fire like a fish vanishing into deeper water.

Dante moved to the man whom Guinizelli had pointed out and said that he was pleased to meet him.

The man replied in Provencal, his native language. The man said, "I am Arnaut Daniel. I cry as I mourn having committed sins, but I feel joy as I think about the Paradise that is to come to me. Please remember my suffering here."

Then he vanished into the flames.

Dante thought, *The sin of lust is a burning sin — one can burn with lust — and therefore the sin of lust is purged with fire. The souls who need to be purged of lust do so by staying in a fire until the sin is purged.*

Chapter 27: Seventh Ledge — Lust (Third Prophetic Dream) (Purgatory)

The time was 6 p.m., and soon the Sun would set.

Dante saw an angel on the other side of the fire. He was singing, "Blessed are the Pure of Heart."

Then the angel said, "Souls, to climb higher on the mountain, you must pass through the fire. Whatever sins are left in you will be purged. Enter the fire, and remember, 'Blessed are the pure in heart, for they shall see God.'"

Statius thought, *Going through fire is the only way to reach the Earthly Paradise.*

Dante was afraid when he learned that he must pass through the fire. He had seen burned bodies at public executions, and he remembered what those bodies looked like.

Virgil thought, *Dante, when you are exiled from Florence, the penalty for coming back to Florence will be death by fire.*

Both Virgil and Statius turned to Dante, and Virgil said, "Remember what we have already been through! We have safely gone through the Inferno! Remember when we rode the back of Geryon! If I kept you safe then, won't I be able to keep you safe now, when we are so much closer to God! Believe me: If you were to stay one thousand years in this fire, it would not singe even a hair on your head. Test the fire. Put the hem of your robe into the fire — the fire will not burn your robe. You will feel pain in the fire, but you will not die. It's time to take this step forward. Don't be afraid. Come with me."

But Dante stood still. He was ashamed, but he stood still.

Virgil was annoyed, but he knew the right way to motivate Dante. He said, "This is the path you must take if you are to see Beatrice."

Just like a dying lover hearing the name of his beloved, Dante was all attention. He was now ready to walk through the fire. He turned toward Virgil, who said, "Let's go."

Virgil asked Statius to bring up the rear, and then Virgil walked into the fire. Dante followed, and although the fire did not burn flesh or clothing, it was so hot that Dante would have eagerly jumped into boiling glass in order to cool down.

Virgil continued to motivate Dante to walk across the fire, saying, "I think I can already see the eyes of Beatrice."

The three poets walked through the fire, and they heard an angel singing, "Come, you blessed of my Father, inherit the kingdom prepared for you from the foundation of the world." These are the words spoken to those who are entering Paradise.

The angel was so bright that Dante had to turn his eyes away from him. The last of the seven P's vanished from Dante's forehead.

The angel then said to the three poets, "The Sun is setting, but do not waste time. Climb as many steps as you are able before the Sun completely sets."

The three poets had climbed only a few steps before the Sun set and Dante's shadow vanished. The stars looked bigger to the three poets than they do to people in the Land of the Living.

The rule of the mountain still held: At night no one can climb higher.

Each poet slept on a stair of his choosing, and Dante was like a goat or lamb protected by two goatherds or shepherds against carnivorous beasts.

Dante dreamed during the hour before dawn; such dreams sometimes bring knowledge of the future.

Dante dreamed that he saw a young, lovely girl picking flowers in a meadow. The girl said, "My name is Leah. I spend my time picking flowers and weaving garlands. I am an artist, and I admire my creations when I look in the mirror. My sister's name is Rachel, and she sits and looks at her eyes in the mirror and never looks away from the mirror. Rachel looks, and I do, and both of us are happy."

Dante thought later, *In the dream, Leah is a doer; she is active. Leah walks through a meadow, gathering flowers to make a garland for herself. Rachel, on the other hand, looks in a mirror all day, contemplating her eyes. Rachel is contemplative. Both are good ways of living life. Although Leah is mostly active, she also contemplates herself in the mirror, but much less often than Rachel. One can be mostly active, or one can be contemplative. In Genesis, Leah and Rachel were the wives of Jacob. If this dream gives knowledge of the future, it means that I will meet two more guides. One, of course, will be Beatrice.*

This is the third dream I have had on the mountain. In the first dream, I dreamed that an eagle carried me higher up the mountain. While I was asleep, Saint Lucia did exactly that. In the second dream, I dreamed about being rescued from a Siren by a Heavenly lady. In this, the third dream, I dreamed about Rachel and Leah.

The Sun rose, and Dante woke up. Both Virgil and Statius were already awake.

Virgil said to Dante, "The eternal happiness that all men search for will — today — be yours." The words also applied to Statius. On this day, the two poets would reach the Earthly Paradise and make the final preparations for Paradise.

The three poets climbed higher, and Dante felt light — so light that he felt as if he were growing wings.

They reached the top of the stairs, and Virgil said to Dante, "You have journeyed through the eternal fire of the Inferno and the temporary — because it will disappear on the Day of Judgment — fire of Purgatory. We have traveled through the places of which I have knowledge. Here my knowledge ends. I have led you here, and I have done that with skill and intelligence. From now on, your Free Will is perfected. You are the master of your desires; they are no longer the master of you. You can no longer desire the wrong things, but only the right things, so let pleasure be your guide. Do what you want to do because that will be the right thing to do. The narrow path to follow lies below; here you are free to wander anywhere. Soon you will see the eyes of Beatrice. You no longer need me to be your guide. Your Will is now Free and perfect, and you are now the King of yourself and you are now the Bishop of yourself. I crown and miter you lord of yourself!"

Dante thought, *I still need a Christian guide, and that guide will be Beatrice. Virgil has taken me as far as he can. Virgil need say no more words to me because his job is done except for delivering me to Beatrice.*

Now that I have passed through Purgatory Proper, my Will is Free. I am no longer shackled by sin. I control my desires; they do not control me. My Free Will is perfect and is unrestrained.

Virgil told me, "I crown and miter you lord of yourself!"

A crown is what a King wears. A miter is what a Bishop wears; it is a headdress. Because I have perfected my Free Will, have been restored to innocence, and am purged of sin, I no longer need a King or a Bishop to guide me. I no longer need the guidance and restraint of Church or State.

I am now my own King and my own Bishop.

Chapter 28: Forest of Eden (Matelda) (Purgatory)

Dante was eager to explore the top of the mountain, and without delay he set forth. On the top of the mountain is a forest. The green leaves made the light soft, without harshness. The scents were soothing, as was the light, steady breeze he felt on his forehead. The breeze always blew with the same intensity, and it always blew in the same direction. Italy is a Mediterranean country that can be hot, but this forest is cool. The sound of birds filled the air as they welcomed the morning. The two poets followed Dante as he moved deeper into the forest.

Dante moved slowly, but soon he was deep in the forest — so deep that he could not see where he had entered it.

Suddenly a stream appeared that blocked his way. The water of the stream was clear — so clear that compared to it the clearest waters in the Land of the Living appear to be clouded. This stream is constantly in shade, and the rays of the Sun and the light that the Moon reflects will never directly touch it.

Dante stopped, and he looked at the land on the other side of the stream. As suddenly as an unexpected miracle, a lady appeared. She was singing, and she was gathering flowers, and she reminded Dante of Leah, one of the two women in his prophetic dream. She was the first of the two female guides whom he would meet.

Dante said to her, "Lady, you are lovely, and your appearance glows with love. Please come nearer so that I can hear and understand the words of your song. You remind me of Proserpine, aka Persephone. She was gathering flowers, when Hades, god of the Underworld, entranced by her beauty, made her his bride and took her with him away from her mother, Ceres, the goddess of agriculture, who mourned. Because Ceres mourned, nothing grew, and Jupiter sent the messenger god Mercury to bring Proserpine back to the Land of the Living. But because she had eaten one-fourth of a pomegranate, she was forced to spend one-fourth of the year with Hades in the underworld, and so Humankind now endures Winter three months of the year, having lost the eternal Spring that Adam and Eve enjoyed in the Garden of Eden."

Moving like a dancer among the red and yellow flowers, the lady turned toward Dante, but she kept her eyes modestly lowered. She walked to the stream that separated Dante from her, and then she raised her eyes and looked at him.

And now Dante was reminded of Venus. The lady's eyes were radiant, and even Venus' eyes could not be so radiant — not even when an arrow of Cupid, her son, lightly scratched her breast when she bent to kiss him, and the arrow made her fall in love with Adonis.

The lady stood on the other side of the stream, and in her hands she arranged the flowers of many colors — flowers that had not grown from seeds.

And Dante hated the stream because it separated him from her. He hated it the way that Leander hated the Hellespont — the water between Europe and Asia Minor — because the water separated him and his beloved, the woman named Hero.

The stream was narrow. Only three feet separated Dante and the lady, but the top of the mountain was a special place, and Dante wanted to cross the stream only when he knew that crossing it was permitted. If only the stream would part like the Red Sea parted for Moses and the Israelites when they fled slavery in Egypt! But it continued flowing.

The lady said, "You three have never been here before. You may be amazed to see me and to hear me singing here in this place that was the cradle of Humankind. To understand why I was singing, think of Psalm 91 — *"Delectasi Me"* or "You Did Delight Me":

"'It is a good thing to give thanks unto the Lord, and to sing praises unto Your name, O most High:

"'To show forth Your lovingkindness in the morning, and Your faithfulness every night,

"'Upon an instrument of ten strings, and upon the psaltery; upon the harp with a solemn sound.

"'For You, Lord, have made me glad through Your work: I will triumph in the works of Your hands.

"'O Lord, how great are Your works! and Your thoughts are very deep.'

"I am rejoicing in the beauty of the Earthly Paradise: this Forest of Eden that is also known as the Garden of Eden. And I am filled with love for its and my Creator.

"You who spoke to me just now, if you have any questions, please ask."

Dante said, "I have heard that no rain falls here, so what is the source of the stream? And what is the source of this breeze?"

Dante thought, *Statius told me earlier that no rain falls here and that the breezes of the Earth's atmosphere have no effect here.*

The lady said, "I will explain the nature of this place. This is where God created Adam, who was supposed to do good and to dwell in this Earthly Paradise, but Adam sinned and he was banished from the garden to work instead of enjoy. You know that God created Adam first and then Eve. God had created the Earthly Paradise for them, and He allowed them to eat all the fruit of the Earthly Paradise except for the fruit of one tree: the Tree of Knowledge of Good and Evil. A serpent came to Eve and tempted her to eat the forbidden fruit. She did eat, and then she persuaded Adam to eat the forbidden fruit. Because of this sin, they were banished from the Earthly Paradise, as were all their descendants. But after death, saved souls can climb to the top of the Mountain of Purgatory and reach once more the Earthly Paradise.

"This is a place where the laws of nature sometimes are not in effect. No storms occur here. The Earthly Paradise is so high that storms cannot reach here. Earthly winds also cannot reach here. The movement of the heavens above us causes the breeze that constantly blows.

"Plants grow here without the need of seeds. All plants grow here in this perfect place. But seeds from plants here travel to the rest of the world. In the Land of the Living, the plants that grow here in profusion will grow only when the soil and weather conditions are right. Here in the Earthly Paradise you can find every species. Here are species that bear fruit of a kind that no man has ever plucked. The Earthly Paradise is a fruitful place.

"The water here does not come from a natural source. The source of the water here is a fountain that is created by the will of God, who causes it to flow without ceasing. The fountain of water divides into two streams. The stream before you has the power to erase the memory of sin's sting when its water is drunk. You will remember many of your sins, but you will know that they have been forgiven, and you will rejoice and be happy that they have been forgiven. Gone will be the pain of the knowledge that you have sinned. This stream is called Lethe, which means 'oblivion.'

"The other stream found here is called Eunoë, which means 'well minded' or 'good memory,' and it also has a special power, but to enjoy the special power of the Eunoë, you must drink first from the Lethe. Drinking from the water of the Eunoë will restore the knowledge of every good deed that you have ever done.

"Let me tell you one more thing. Poets of long ago sang of a Golden Age. They fell asleep on Parnassus, the mountain of the Muses, and dreamed of this place. The Golden Age they dreamed and sang of was the time when Humankind lived here. Here, Humankind was without sin and without guilt, and here were clear water and every fruit. The nectar that ancient poets sang of was and is found here."

Dante looked back at Virgil and Statius, two of the ancient poets who sang of the Golden Age, to see what they thought of the lady's words about them. The two poets were smiling.

Then he looked again at the lovely lady.

Chapter 29: Forest of Eden — Pageant of Revelation (Purgatory)

The lady then sang, "Blessed are they whose sins are forgiven."

Dante thought, *The sins of anyone who is allowed to drink from the stream named Lethe are forgiven.*

The lady began to walk along the stream. Dante followed her, and the two poets followed him. She walked like a beautiful woman who was at home in Nature. She walked upstream with small steps, and Dante walked slowly with short steps so that he did not outpace her.

The stream curved, and Dante faced East. The lady stopped and said to Dante, "Look and listen."

The sky brightened and at first Dante thought that lightning had flashed, but the brightness did not diminish but instead increased. Dante also heard a melody.

The beauty of what he was experiencing made him angry at Eve, whose sin banished Humankind from the Earthly Paradise until such time as a saved soul could climb the Mountain of Purgatory. If not for Eve, Dante could have enjoyed the Earthly Paradise during all of his previous and future life.

Here was the beginning of the happiness of Paradise, and Dante longed for the greater happiness to come.

The light grew brighter among the green leaves, and the sound grew louder into a chant.

Dante prayed to the Muses — the Holy Virgins — for help in relating what he was seeing and hearing: *If I have labored long and hard to write good poetry, for a reward I want to write better poetry on a better subject. Let the waters of the sacred stream of you Muses pour upon me, and let Urania, the Muse of astronomy — and thus of Heavenly things — inspire me as I write.*

Dante saw what appeared to be seven golden trees, but he was mistaken because of the objects' distance from him. When the objects came closer, he saw that they were seven golden candlesticks.

He also heard the word *Hosanna* — "Save, we pray!" — being sung.

Above the gold of the candlesticks was a brilliant light.

In amazement, Dante turned and looked at Virgil, who answered his glance with his own look of amazement.

Virgil thought, *I am not a Christian. I have no knowledge of what I am seeing.*

Dante turned back.

The religious procession moved slowly, and Dante looked at the seven golden candlesticks. The lady, impatient, said to him, "Why are you looking only at the seven golden candlesticks? Look also at what follows them!"

Dante then looked past the candlesticks, and he saw a spectacular pageant, and he realized that he was looking at a religious procession in which Heavenly figures dressed themselves in allegorical guises. Some of the Heavenly figures may have actually been themselves. Each guise, including the candlesticks, had a religious and specifically Christian meaning.

Dante thought, *The seven golden candlesticks are an image from the Book of Revelation. The seven candlesticks can be interpreted as representing the gifts of God's spirit: Wisdom, Understanding, Counsel, Might, Knowledge, Piety, and Fear of (aka Reverence for) the Lord.*

Following the candlesticks were 24 figures dressed in white. The whiteness was reflected in the stream to Dante's left, and Dante saw his left side reflected there. He moved as close to the stream as he could, and then he looked at the pageant.

The seven candlesticks advanced, and in the sky they left seven streams that were the seven colors of the rainbow. The pennants of color stretched further back than Dante could see. The width of each stream of color was fully 10 strides.

Next came 24 elders, marching two by two, and wearing crowns of lilies. The 24 elders sang to the Virgin Mary, "Blessed be You of all of the daughters of Adam. Blessed be your beauty forever."

Dante thought, *The 24 elders represent the books of the Old Testament in the Vulgate Bible of Saint Jerome, counting the books of the 12 minor prophets as one book. Saint Jerome translated the Bible into Latin in what is known as the Vulgate Bible. The word "vulgate" is Latin, and it can be translated as "widespread." Of course, the purpose of translating the Bible into Latin was the same as that of other translations: to make it more available to more people.*

It is important that these figures who represent the books of the Old Testament are praising the Virgin Mary. This shows their prophetic power.

The 24 elders are dressed in white, a color that is symbolic of illuminating faith.

These are the 12 minor prophets: Hosea, Joel, Amos, Obadiah, Jonah, Michah, Nahum, Habakkuk, Zephaniah, Haggai, Zechariah, and Malachi.

Following these 24 elders came four beasts that were wearing forest-green crowns. Each beast had six wings, each of which was covered with eyes.

Dante thought, *These beasts represent the four authors of the gospels: Matthew, Mark, Luke, and John. Why are these four authors represented as beasts? The image comes from Revelation 4:6-8 and from Ezekiel 1:4-14. The crowns of green signify hope.*

The four beasts were spaced around a two-wheeled chariot that was drawn by a Griffin — which is part eagle and part lion — with wings raised high. The part of the Griffin that was an eagle was gold, and the part of the Griffin that was a lion was white with dark red marks.

Dante thought, *A Griffin is a figure from mythology; it has two natures because it is half-eagle and half-lion. The Griffin is a symbol of Jesus, Who also has two natures: Jesus is fully human, yet fully divine.*

The chariot was splendid — more splendid than the triumphal chariot ridden in by Scipio Africanus, who finally conquered the Carthaginian general Hannibal, who had crossed the Alps with his elephants in order to war against the Romans. It was also more splendid than the triumphal chariot ridden in by Caesar Augustus, the first Roman Emperor. It was even more splendid than the chariot of the Sun ridden in by Phaeton when he could not control the horses and nearly burned up the planet Earth — Jupiter destroyed him in order to save the Earth.

Dante thought, *The chariot drawn by the Griffin is a symbol that represents the Church.*

Beside the left wheel of the chariot were four ladies, all of whom were dressed in purple, and one of whom had three eyes. All four ladies were dancing.

Dante thought, *These ladies are symbolic of the four virtues from classical antiquity: Prudence, Temperance, Justice, and Fortitude. These are known as the cardinal virtues. The lady with three eyes symbolizes Prudence. Why? Prudence can see the past, the present, and the future.*

Circling in a dance by the right wheel of the chariot were three ladies. One lady was fiery red. One lady was emerald green. One lady was as white as newly fallen snow. Sometimes, the white lady led the dance, and sometimes the red lady led the dance.

Dante thought, *These women at the sides of the wheels of the chariot are symbolic of the three Christian virtues: Faith (White), Hope (Green), and Charity (Red). These are known as the theological virtues.*

Then came two aged men in the procession. One aged man was wearing the garments of a follower of Hippocrates, a healer of the ill. The other aged man bore a sharp sword that frightened Dante.

Dante thought, *Side by side, these two figures represent the healing physician Luke (beloved physician and author of the Acts of the Apostles) and Paul (author of the major epistles) with his frightening, sin-wounding sword.*

Behind the two aged men came four humble men.

Dante thought, *These figures represent the other epistle writers: Peter, James, John, and Jude.*

Then came one old man by himself. The old man appeared to be dreaming, and his face was inspired.

Dante thought, *This is John the Divine, the author of the Book of Revelation.*

All of these seven figures at the end of the procession were dressed in white and were wearing wreaths with red roses and other red flowers, giving the effect — from far away — of flames. When the chariot was opposite Dante, thunder boomed, and each part of the procession stopped at exactly the same time.

Dante thought, *God revealed himself in three stages during Biblical times: 1) The Hebrew Testament, aka Old Testament, 2) The four Gospels (Matthew, Mark, Luke, and John), 3) The later books of the New Testament. In the pageant, I have seen figures representing all of these books.*

Chapter 30: Forest of Eden — Exit of Virgil; Entrance of Beatrice (Purgatory)

When the seven candlesticks and the rest of the procession had stopped, the 24 elders who followed them all turned to the chariot, which was a symbol of the Church, and one of the 24 elders sang, "Come, soul wedded to Christ, from Lebanon." The other elders then joined their voices to his, as he sang the words three times.

When the Day of Judgment arrives, all the dead, newly rejoined with their bodies, will sing, "Hallelujah." With sound and feeling just like that, a hundred angels above the chariot sang, "Blessed are You Who is Coming." They followed this by singing, "Give Lilies with Both Hands," as they tossed flowers into the air.

Dante thought, *This is a major compliment to Virgil. The first words the angels sang are, in Latin, "Benedictus Qui Venis," which is very close to Matthew 21:9: "Benedictus Qui Venit": "Blessed is He Who is Coming." The next words the angels sang are, in Latin, "Manibus, O Date Lilia Plenis," which is a direct quotation from Book 6 of Virgil's Aeneid. For the angels to sing both a variant of sacred scripture and in almost the same breath sing some words from Virgil's masterpiece has to make Virgil happy.*

Sometimes, at the beginning of dawn, a rose color appears in the East, and the starry air is remarkably clear, and then the Sun appears in a mist that allows the eye to look at it without harm.

Like the appearance of such a Sun, a lady appeared as angels tossed flowers that covered the chariot. The lady wore a white veil, a green cloak, and a red gown. She also wore an olive crown. Dante recognized the lady: Beatrice.

Dante thought, *The purpose of the procession I just saw was to prepare for the entrance of Beatrice, who is wearing three colors that have religious significance. The three colors represent the theological virtues: Faith, Hope, and Charity. In addition, the olive crown symbolizes wisdom.*

As soon as Dante saw Beatrice, his long-time love for her — love he had felt for her since he first saw her when she was eight years old and he was nine — returned to him. He had felt that love from the time he first saw her until she had died at the age of 24.

Dante the Pilgrim turned to his left to talk to Virgil just like a child who is frightened or who needs comforting runs to his or her mother. He wanted to say to Virgil, "Every drop of my blood is filled with love for Beatrice. I recognize signs of the ancient flame."

Dante the Poet thought, *The second sentence of what I wanted to say to Virgil is a direct quote from Virgil's* Aeneid — *"Agnosco veteris vestigia flammae." Dido, the Queen of Carthage, says these words when she falls in love with Aeneas, the Trojan warrior who had survived the fall of Troy and was destined to become an important ancestor of the Roman people.*

But Virgil was not present. His job was done, and he had started the journey back to Limbo. Now that he had delivered Dante to Beatrice, he did not stay around, and he did not say goodbye.

Even though Dante was in the Earthly Paradise, aka the Garden of Eden, and even though delights surrounded him, still he cried. He had delivered the safekeeping of his body and soul to Virgil, and he had not had the opportunity to thank or even say goodbye to him. Virgil had washed the stains of Dante's tears away at the bottom of the Mountain of Purgatory, but now Dante cried.

Beatrice told him, "Dante, do not cry. Or, rather, do not cry yet. You are crying because Virgil has left you. Soon, you will have a better reason to cry. Do not cry now."

Beatrice was standing on the chariot the way an admiral stands on a ship. An admiral calls the men to work, and Beatrice was calling on Dante to do the work of repenting his sins.

Dante turned and looked at Beatrice. She was wearing a veil, but Dante could still see the expression on her face. She was stern as she looked at him. The words she had to say to Dante were not intended to be pleasant to hear, although they were necessary for Dante's salvation.

Beatrice said to him, "Yes! Look at me! I am Beatrice. Finally, you have climbed the mountain! Have you learned yet that this is the way to eternal happiness?"

Dante was ashamed and looked down. He saw his reflection in the stream, and he looked away from his reflection.

Dante was like a guilty child being judged by his or her mother. He was miserable, and she was stern. Even a loving mother can be stern when sternness is needed.

When Beatrice had finished speaking, all of the angels sang the first eight lines of Psalm 31:

"In You, O Lord, do I put my trust; let me never be ashamed: deliver me in Your righteousness.

"Bow down Your ear to me; deliver me speedily: be You my strong rock, for a house of defence to save me.

"For You are my rock and my fortress; therefore for Your name's sake lead me, and guide me.

"Pull me out of the net that they have laid privily for me: for You are my strength.

"Into Your hand I commit my spirit: You have redeemed me, O Lord God of truth.

"I have hated them who regard lying vanities: but I trust in the Lord.

"I will be glad and rejoice in Your mercy: for You have considered my trouble; You have known my soul in adversities;

"And have not shut me up into the hand of the enemy: You have put my feet in a large room."

Figuratively, Dante the Pilgrim was standing in a large room.

Just like the snow of the Apennines, a mountain range in Italy, will melt when air from equatorial Africa makes its way over it, so Dante's heart was chilled when he heard Beatrice criticize him, but it melted when he heard the angels plead for him as they said to Beatrice, "Lady, why are you so hard on him?" The ice that had been within Dante melted and turned into tears.

The angels were compassionate, but Beatrice was not yet compassionate. She told the angels, "Your eyes see Paradise, yet no act on Earth is hidden from you. Even though I am now talking to you, the purpose of my words is to make this man who is now weeping realize just how guilty of sin he is.

"This man was gifted. Not only was he gifted through heredity, but also he was gifted through the workings of God. From an early age, he had great gifts. If he had used his gifts the way they ought to have been used, he would have seen enormous benefit.

"A rich soil when cultivated will bring forth much fruit, but a rich soil when uncultivated will bring forth many weeds. This man did not cultivate his gifts. He let bad seeds flourish.

"At one time, he loved me, and I loved the revelation of God, but when my physical body died, and I lost life but acquired Life, this man abandoned all thought of me and chased after others. He was unfaithful and did not do those things he ought to have done.

"I had left behind my body and had become all spirit, and yet he stopped loving me and he found no pleasure in thinking about me. He wandered from the path that leads to good and followed the path that leads to evil. He pursued things that pretended to be good and that promised much more than they were capable of delivering.

"I did not abandon him. I knew that his soul was in danger. Through prayer, I won for him truthful dreams and visions so that he could be inspired to pursue the path that leads to good. He refused to be inspired. Eventually, he became so evil that the only way to get him back on the correct path was to show him the Damned in the Inferno.

"To make this happen, I, a saved soul, visited Hell, and in Limbo I pleaded, in tears, to Virgil to be his guide and to lead him here. This man here cannot be allowed to drink of Lethe yet. To allow him to do that would be a violation of the laws of God. First, he must cry tears of true repentance."

The angels thought, *Beatrice knows what Dante must do. Christians believe that anyone can be saved — God offers salvation to all, not just to a few. However, the way that people can be saved can vary, although it will always involve confessing and repenting their sins. God reaches people in many ways. In Dante's case, God reaches him through Beatrice. Beatrice is able to show Dante the way to Paradise. Beatrice is a harsh judge for Dante at this point. To be ready for his journey to and through Paradise, Dante must confess and repent his sins. Beatrice is stern as she talks about the bad things that Dante has done and about the good things that he has failed to do. Beatrice is taking her job as guide seriously, as she should. Beatrice wants Dante to end up in Paradise rather than in the Inferno. Beatrice is working hard to help Dante be saved.*

Chapter 31: Forest of Eden — Lethe (Purgatory)

Beatrice spoke to Dante, "You there on the other side of the stream Lethe, speak. Isn't what I have said true? You must confess that you have sinned." Beatrice's words had been like the edge of a sword before — they cut. But now her words were like the point of a sword — they pierced.

Dante stood before her. He felt paralyzed. He felt confused. He moved his lips, but no sound came forth.

Beatrice continued, "What are you thinking? Answer me. The bitterness of your sins has not yet ceased because you have not yet drunk from this stream. Do you confess that you have sinned?"

I still have the bitter memories of the sins I have done and of the good things that I have not done. Many people — those who are not pathological — remember with bitterness things that they have done in the past but should not have done. They also remember things that they have not done but should have done. Sometimes, these bitter memories keep us awake at night.

Finally, Dante was able to force a word from between his lips. He confessed, miserably and with full knowledge of his guilt, "Yes."

An arrow launched by a crossbow that breaks has little force, and so Dante, racked by guilt and with tears and sighs, launched his "Yes" with so little force that only a lip reader could know what he had said.

Beatrice said to him, "You loved me, and I tried to lead you to the Eternal Good, but you did not follow. What obstacles lay in your way that interfered with your pursuit of the Eternal Good? What did you find so desirable that you pursued them instead of the Eternal Good?"

Dante sighed, and weeping, he confessed, "After I lost sight of you, I pursued things that offer false joys, things that were offered to me by the world, things that led away from the Eternal Good."

Beatrice said, "Your confession is heard. But if you had not spoken, or if you had denied your sins, your sins would still be known by God, the Judge who knows everything."

The angels thought, *Dante has learned from the trip that he has taken through the Afterlife: Dante has learned to take responsibility for his sins. This is something that the sinners in the Inferno did not do. Dante has also learned to repent his sins. This is also something that the sinners in the Inferno did not do. Many people become defensive when they are charged with something serious. Instead of admitting their guilt, they blame someone or something else: Love made them do it, or a book made them do it, or the Devil made them do it. Instead of blaming someone or something else, Dante simply admits that he is guilty — he made himself do it.*

Beatrice continued, "But when a sinner confesses his sins, the punishment in this court is lessened.

"But you still need to feel the shame of the sins you committed. That way, when you return to the Land of the Living, and the Siren sings for you, you will be strong enough to resist the Siren's song.

"Listen to me. Learn how my flesh, which is buried, was intended to teach you to take a better path than the one you freely chose to take.

"You never saw anything more beautiful — not in nature, not in art — than the living flesh that made up my body. That flesh is now dead and turned to dust.

"Once you knew that my living flesh could die and turn to dust, how could you pursue anything else that had only temporary value and temporary beauty? You should have learned from my death to turn your attention to the things that last. Instead of physical beauty, you should have pursued spiritual beauty."

The angels thought, *What are the eternal things — what are the good and beautiful things that last? What are some possible answers? They are such things as virtuous love, truth, and beauty. These things appear in the virtuous love we experience on Earth, and these things are part of great works of art. These things are important in Paradise.*

Beatrice continued, "When I died, you should have rushed to pursue spiritual beauty. You had suffered one blow. Why love another pretty woman or other temporary beauty and set yourself up for another blow?

"A fledgling waits and suffers a blow from a second arrow, but the mature bird sets itself in flight and does not let itself by used by a second arrow as a target."

Dante stood before Beatrice like a child silently standing before a mother who has scolded the child. The child knows that he or she is guilty, and the child feels sorry. So did Dante.

Beatrice said to Dante, "If simply hearing my words causes you grief, raise your beard and look at me and see what will cause you greater grief."

And when Dante, an adult man who had pursued glittery trivialities the way that a child would, raised his eyes and looked at Beatrice, he saw that she was facing the Griffin — the being that has two natures.

Beatrice was still wearing a veil, and she was still on the land across the stream, and she looked more beautiful than she ever had while she was still alive on Earth, when she was the most beautiful woman in the world.

Dante felt guilty. After Beatrice had died, he had loved some things, but now he hated them. His guilt overwhelmed him, and he fainted.

When he regained consciousness, the lady whom he had first seen in the Earthly Paradise was over him and telling him, "Hold on tight to me."

Dante was in the stream, the lady was walking on the water, and she pulled him across the stream with ease.

As he was being drawn across the stream, he heard the sweet singing of some words from Psalm 51: "Cleanse me of sin."

The lady dipped Dante into the stream, and he drank, and then she drew him out of the stream, cleansed of his sins.

The four ladies who are symbolic of four virtues from classical antiquity — Prudence, Temperance, Justice, and Fortitude — came dancing to Dante and raised and joined their hands over him.

They said to him, "When you first arrived on the Mountain of Purgatory, you saw us as four stars. Now we are here before you and appearing to you as ladies. Even from the time before Beatrice was born, we were meant to be her handmaids. Now we will lead you to her eyes. The other three ladies, who were at the sides of the wheels of the chariot and who are symbolic of three Christian virtues — Faith, Hope, and Charity — see more deeply than we do and will help you to see more deeply than we can."

The four ladies led Dante to Beatrice and the Griffin, and Beatrice looked at the Griffin.

The four ladies told Dante, "Look deeply into Beatrice's eyes. These are the eyes that made you love Beatrice."

Dante looked at Beatrice's eyes. Reflected in her eyes was the Griffin, who has two natures that are symbolic of Jesus, who has a divine nature and a human nature, and who has both natures at the same time.

Dante looked, and he saw first one nature and then the other, but he was incapable of seeing both natures at the same time, although they were there and Beatrice saw them at the same time.

Dante was delighted and amazed by what he saw, and he wanted to continue to be delighted and amazed.

The three ladies who are symbolic of the theological virtues came to Dante and said to Beatrice, "Turn and look at Dante. He has come very far to look at you. Please remove the veil that covers your mouth. Smile, and allow him to see more of your beauty."

Beatrice removed her veil, and she smiled, and Dante saw beauty that he was unable to describe even with his poetic gifts that are destined to last through millennia.

Beatrice had the beauty of Revelation, and she had the beauty of Salvation.

Chapter 32: Forest of Eden — Pageant of Church History (Purgatory)

Dante stared at Beatrice. She had died in 1290, and he had 10 years of longing to look at her to satisfy. Sight was the only sense he used, and he used it so intently that he was oblivious of his other senses.

He stared at her smile, and he was as attracted to Beatrice as he had been when she was still alive.

But then he heard the three ladies complain, "He should not look so intently." Dante was not yet ready to look intently at Beatrice and all she represented about Paradise.

Dante was blinded like someone who had stared at the Sun. His blindness lasted only briefly.

He regained his sight and was able to look at things that seemed dim compared to what he had been staring at, and he saw that the spectacular procession had moved. The golden candlesticks, 24 elders, and all the rest had started making a right-turn-about. The procession had come from the East, but having moved it was now facing the Sun. The seven candlesticks were still in front.

Like soldiers, those in front had moved and turned first, and now the seven ladies took their places by the wheels of the chariot, and the Griffin began to pull it. The Griffin easily pulled the chariot; not a single feather of the Griffin was ruffled.

Statius, Dante, and the lady of the Earthly Paradise moved behind the chariot as it turned.

They walked in the Earthly Paradise, which was empty of living Humankind except for Dante because of the sin of Eve, who had listened to the snake, sinned, and given cause for living humans to be banished.

The procession continued moving, and Beatrice got out of the chariot. The procession murmured, "Adam," the name of he who had been the partner of Eve in sin, and the procession surrounded a tree with branches but without leaves or fruit.

The tree was very tall, and the taller it was, the more its branches spread. This tree resembled the tree on the ledge of the gluttonous, and so Dante knew that this was the Tree of Knowledge of Good and Evil, as described in Genesis. This is why the procession had murmured Adam's name.

The members of the procession sang, "Blessed are you, Griffin, for you did not eat of the bark of this tree. The bark tastes sweet, but it causes illness."

The Griffin replied, "And so I preserved the seed of righteousness."

Beatrice thought, *The bark of this tree represents the things that religious people ought to resist, especially including material wealth. Jesus lived in holy poverty, and so he was able to concentrate on spiritual wealth rather than on material wealth.*

The Griffin had pulled the chariot with pieces of wood that made a pole with a crossbar that formed a cross. Now the Griffin tied the pole to the tree, which grew purple blooms.

Beatrice thought, *This tree represents the Roman Empire, as shown by the height of the tree. Tall trees are used in Scripture as symbols of the great empires of Assyria and Babylon. This tree is higher than the highest trees of India and so the Roman Empire is superior to the empires of India. When Empire and Church are properly connected and related to each other, things can bloom. The tree had been barren, but now that it is connected again with the Cross, all is well. The true Cross was made of wood taken from the Tree of Knowledge of Good and Evil, and so those pieces of wood are now united again with the tree. The tree's blooms are purple, representing the blood of Jesus when he died to save Humankind.*

The procession began to sing a hymn that Dante did not recognize because that hymn is not sung on Earth — and Dante fell asleep. In falling asleep, he missed experiencing what else the procession did.

He woke up when a voice called, "What are you doing there? Arise!"

Dante thought, *Matthew 17 recounts that the disciples Peter, John, and James witnessed the transfigured Christ. They fell trembling to the ground until Jesus touched them and said, "Arise!"*

Dante looked up, and he saw that the lady of the Earthly Paradise was bent over him. He asked, "Where is Beatrice?" He was afraid that she had gone.

The lady replied, "She is sitting on the roots under the tree's newborn leaves. The procession has left with the Griffin and gone to Paradise."

The lady may have said more words, but Dante did not hear them because he was paying attention to Beatrice.

She was guarding the chariot that the Griffin had left connected to the tree.

The seven ladies were with her, and they were holding the seven golden candlesticks that had led the procession.

Beatrice told Dante, "For a short time, you will continue to dwell in the Land of the Living, and then you will be with me forever in Paradise. You will be saved. You will not be sentenced to eternal torment in the Inferno.

"Watch carefully now. You will see things that I want you to remember and to tell the living."

Dante wanted to be of service to Beatrice. He watched carefully.

An eagle swooped to earth and attacked the tree, tearing off its bark and its blooms. Then the eagle attacked the chariot, which resembled a ship in a storm, battered by waves.

Dante thought, *The chariot is a symbol of the Church, and the eagle is a symbol of the Roman Empire. The Roman legions carried standards into battle. The standards were poles with insignia or symbols at the top. The Roman standards often had the figure of an eagle at the top. Here I am seeing a representation of the persecutions of the early Christians by Roman emperors such as Nero and Diocletian.*

Then a skinny fox jumped into the chariot. Whatever food it fed on did not nourish it. Beatrice chased the fox away and accused it of abominations.

Dante thought, *The fox is a symbol of the early heresies that the Church had to confront. The Church was successful in resisting the heresies, which provide no nourishment to Christians. A heresy is an opinion that differs from orthodox doctrine. For example, a disbelief in immortality is a heresy.*

Again the eagle swooped down. It had golden feathers, and it left a few golden feathers in the chariot. Dante heard a voice from Heaven cry, "My little ship, the cargo you carry is not worthy of you."

Dante thought, *A ship is often used as a symbol for the Church, so that is what the voice is referring to here. This scene is a reference to the document known as the Donation of Constantine. Constantine was the first Christian Roman emperor. When he moved from Rome to the city of Constantinople, he gave much power and many material possessions to the Pope. Constantine deliberately moved East in order to reward Pope Sylvester I with power and possessions because Pope Sylvester I had cured him of leprosy. This Donation of Constantinople corrupted many Popes and the Church. The Donation of Constantine caused a crisis in the Church because suddenly the Popes became more concerned about money and power than they were concerned about God. In fact, the Donation of Constantine is having bad effects in Florence and Rome 1,000 years after Constantine gave his Donation to the Church. Constantine died in 337, and Constantinople is named after him.*

Beatrice thought, *Dante is mostly right. The golden feathers do represent material riches. When the Church began to pursue material riches rather than spiritual riches, corruption began. It started slowly at first. However, the Donation of Constantine document that Dante believes in is a forgery, as will be proven after Dante dies. Still, Dante got the main point right.*

Then a dragon came up from the ground between the wheels of the chariot. It drove its tail up through the floor of the chariot, causing a division in it. The dragon wandered away slowly, as if it might return and do more damage to the chariot.

Dante thought, *This represents the schisms that have divided the Church. One such schism is between the eastern and the western Church. And Mohammad started another schism with Islam.*

Then the chariot appeared to grow feathers. Possibly, the feathers grew with good intentions, but they soon covered the chariot.

Dante thought, *People such as Constantine gave material riches to the Church with good intentions. Constantine did not mean to hurt the Church. He meant only to help the Church. But once the Church got a taste for material riches, it wanted more and more. This led to corruption — lots of corruption.*

Then the chariot changed into a monster. Seven heads grew on it. Three heads grew on the pole of the chariot, and a head grew on each of the chariot's four corners. The heads on the pole of the chariot had two horns each; the other heads had one horn each.

Dante thought, *The heads are the Seven Deadly Sins.*

Then Dante saw a half-dressed whore sitting on the monster that had been the chariot and looking sluttishly around. A giant stood by her, and he and she kissed. But when the whore cast a sluttish glance at Dante, the giant became enraged and beat her. Then he dragged her and the monster that had been the chariot away out of sight.

Beatrice thought, *Dante can tell other people what he sees here. The telling can provide knowledge to the living, if they will listen to Dante. But he and they will not know the proper interpretation of this until it occurs in the future.*

The whore represents the Pope. When the whore casts an inappropriate glance at Dante, the whore represents Pope Boniface VIII, who will get Dante exiled. The giant represents King Philip IV, aka Philip the Fair, of France. In 1303, Philip had his bullies beat up Pope Boniface VIII, who died a month after the attack.

When the giant drags the whore and the chariot out of sight, this represents Philip the Fair rigging the election of Pope Clement V in 1305 so that he could move the Papal Seat to France instead of Rome. Seven Popes, all of whom were French, will stay in Avignon, France, from 1309 to 1377, when Pope Gregory XI will move the Papacy back to Rome.

For a while, King Philip IV of France will have the power, not the Popes. The Holy Roman Emperor should have power over secular matters and the Pope should have power over spiritual matters. Both men should be good men, and they should not engage in a power struggle.

Chapter 33: Forest of Eden — Purgation Completed (Purgatory)

The ladies sang words from Psalm 79, words that mourned the destruction of Jerusalem: "O God, the heathen are come into Your inheritance; Your holy temple have they defiled; they have laid Jerusalem on heaps." Beatrice listened.

The ladies and Beatrice were mourning the vicissitudes of the Church that they had just witnessed. Beatrice mourned as much as Mary had mourned at the foot of the cross.

The ladies finished singing and Beatrice stood up. Glowing like fire, she prophesied, using the words that Jesus spoke to his disciples when he announced his resurrection: "A little while, and you shall not see me: and again, a little while, and you shall see me."

The Church undergoes vicissitudes in the short run, but the Church shall triumph in the long run.

The seven ladies began walking, Beatrice followed, and with a nod she bade Dante, Statius, and the lady of the Earthly Paradise to follow her.

She had walked only a few paces when she said to Dante, "Walk quickly, so if I have anything to say to you, you will be close enough to me to hear me."

Dante walked quickly, and she asked him, "Why aren't you asking me any questions now that I have arrived?"

Dante felt like someone who knew that he was before a superior and could barely speak, and he said with barely voiced words, "You know what I need to know, and you can tell me what I need to know."

Beatrice replied, "From now on, I want you to speak freely like someone without fear and shame. Speak like someone who is not dreaming.

"You saw the dragon break the chariot. Know that the chariot was broken, but that it shall be fixed. Whoever is guilty of breaking the chariot will be punished. For so serious a sin, God is unwilling to be swayed by pitiful attempts at reconciliation. The eagle that you saw shedding feathers will have true heirs, eventually."

Beatrice thought, *Dante may not understand me, but I know that the Church will be made whole again. I also know that although the Holy Roman Empire has no true emperor now, someday a true secular leader will arise.*

Beatrice continued, "I am telling you these things because I can see the future. I know what will happen. I know that nothing can prevent it from happening. I know that the numbers five hundred, ten, and five are important to the emissary who will kill the giant and the giant's whore."

Dante thought, *The Roman numerals for 500, 10, and 5 are L, X, and V. Rearrange these letters and we have the Latin word LVX, or LUX, which means "leader." But Beatrice can speak clearly, and here she is not speaking clearly, so this may not be what she means.*

Beatrice continued, "My prophecy may not be clear to you. I know that my words are unclear, as were the words of the difficult-to-solve riddle of the Sphinx and of the obscure oracles of the Greek goddess Themis, personification of justice, law, and divine order. But soon events shall make clear the meaning of my words without the bad consequences that followed some of the prophecies of the ancients.

"Listen carefully to my words. Repeat them to those who are living and who need to learn that life is a race with death as the finish line.

"And when you write, don't leave out the tree that you saw despoiled twice, once when the eagle attacked the tree, and once when the giant detached the chariot from the tree.

"Whoever harms the tree sins against God.

"Adam tasted the fruit of the Tree of Knowledge of Good and Evil. Because of that, he was expelled from the Earthly Paradise. He lived outside of the Earthly Paradise for 930 years, and he waited in Limbo for 4,302 years until the Harrowing of Hell.

"Since Adam and Eve tasted the fruit, the tree has grown to a great height, and its branches are inverted toward the top to make the fruit inaccessible to Humankind.

"If you think correctly, you can understand why the tree had these two strange characteristics and why its fruit is forbidden to Humankind. Some things cannot be completely understood by Humankind, and one of them is the mystery of evil. Thus, God was just when He denied this fruit to Humankind. But Adam and Eve ate of the fruit, as God — Who knows everything — knew that they would do. So now Humankind must use its knowledge and its reason and what it learns from revelation to determine to the best of its ability what is the right thing to do and to do it.

"I can see that you do not fully understand my words, but I want you to bring back to the Land of the Living at least the part that you can understand."

Dante replied, "I will do as you ask. I cannot forget your words. They are imprinted on me the way that a seal imprints itself when pressed into wax.

"But why is it so hard for me to understand your words? They fly above my mind. I try to see them, and they fly out of my sight."

Beatrice replied, "I speak in this way so that you may see the error you committed on Earth after my physical body died, when you pursued false paths instead of the true path that God and I wanted you to follow. Your path separated yourself from God and me.

"And I want you to understand that the false paths of Humankind are far from the true path of God."

Dante said, "I cannot remember having ever separated myself from you. I have no guilty conscience."

Beatrice said, "You have drunk from the stream of Lethe, and you have forgotten what you did after my physical body died. The fact that you have forgotten shows that what you did was sinful.

"From now on, however, I will speak more clearly so that you may understand me."

The Sun was overhead now, and the seven ladies stopped walking. Ahead of them was a marvelous sight. A fountain of water shot up and divided itself into two streams.

Dante asked, "What is this water that divides itself into two streams?"

Beatrice replied, "Ask Matelda. She can explain."

The lady of the Earthly Paradise said, "I have already explained that to him, as well as other things. This knowledge is not sinful, and drinking from the stream Lethe will not have taken that knowledge from him."

Beatrice said, "Other things may have crowded out this knowledge from his mind."

Beatrice thought, *My reproach of him, and the spectacular pageant of the vicissitudes of the Church that he recently saw, are both important things that may have made him forget what he had previously learned.*

Beatrice continued, "The fountain divides into two streams: the Lethe and the Eunoë. You have already drunk from the Lethe. Now drink from the Eunoë so that it may revive the knowledge of every good deed that you have ever done in your life.

"Matelde, lead him to the Eunoë, as you lead all saved souls."

Matelda took Dante by the hand and said to Statius, "You come, too."

Statius drank from the stream, and pure, renewed, and immaculate, he rose to his place in Paradise.

Dante drank from the stream.

Years later, Dante the Poet, writing about his experience on the Mountain of Purgatory, wrote, "Reader, I wish I had more space in which I would write about drinking from the stream. But I have carefully planned the writing of the three parts of my *Comedy*: *Inferno*, *Purgatory*, and *Paradise*, and I have used up my allotted number of words for the *Purgatory*. Art must be disciplined."

Dante rose from the stream pure, renewed, and immaculate, and he was eager to rise as Statius had. He was ready to rise to the stars.

Afterword

Now that you have read this retelling in prose of Dante's great epic poem *Purgatory*, you have a good but basic understanding of it.

Now go and read the real thing. I recommend the translation by Mark Musa. The translation by John Ciardi is also very good.

The translations in this volume are taken from works in the public domain and are sometimes altered to make the language more modern.

The translation of *"Te Lucis Ante Terminum"* — "Before the End of the Light" — in this volume is by J. M. Neale (1818-1866).

The translation of *"Te Deum Laudamus"* is by Martin Luther.

The translation of the song sung by the Lustful on ledge nine is by John David Chambers (1805-1893).

Appendix A: Background Information

• Who was Dante Alighieri?

Dante, of course, is the author of *The Divine Comedy*. He was born a Roman Catholic in Florence in 1265 C.E. He died of malaria in Ravenna, Italy, in 1321 (the night of Sept. 13-14). He remains buried in Ravenna, although an empty tomb in Florence is dedicated to him. Dante is known for his ability as a world-class poet, for his interest in politics, and for being exiled from Florence. In a way, he remains exiled from Florence, as his body is not in a tomb in Florence.

• What is *The Divine Comedy* in essence?

The Divine Comedy tells about Dante's imaginative journey through the afterlife. Dante finds himself in a dark wood of error, and his guide, Virgil, the author of the Roman epic the *Aeneid*, takes Dante through the Inferno (Hell), and up the Mountain of Purgatory to the Forest of Eden. There Beatrice, Dante's beloved who died early in life, takes over as Dante's guide, and the two ascend the spheres of Paradise, until finally Dante, with the aid of another guide and of the Virgin Mary, is able to see God face to face. These three parts of Dante's imaginative journey make up the three parts of *The Divine Comedy*: the *Inferno*, the *Purgatory*, and the *Paradise*.

In *The Divine Comedy*, Dante tells the reader how to achieve Paradise. In addition, the epic is a love story. A woman saves Dante.

• How long does the journey in *The Divine Comedy* take?

Considering all the distance that is traveled, it doesn't take long at all. It begins on the night before Good Friday and ends on Easter Wednesday of the year 1300, when Dante was 35 years old (midway through his three score and ten years). The journey takes roughly five and a half days. The year 1300 is significant other than being the midpoint of Dante's life. In 1300, spiritual repentance and spiritual renewal were major themes of the Catholic Church's first Holy Year.

• What is the scope of *The Divine Comedy*?

Herman Melville, author of *Moby Dick*, once said that in order to write a mighty book, an author needs to choose a mighty theme. By choosing the afterlife as his theme, Dante chose a mighty theme. He writes about the Inferno and how sins are punished, about Purgatory and how sins are purged, and about Paradise and how good souls are rewarded. In doing this, he writes about many themes that are important to people of his time and to people of our time and to people of any time: religion, God, poetry, politics, etc.

• **Is *The Divine Comedy* universal?**

"Universal" means applicable to anyone, at any time, and anywhere. Yes, *The Divine Comedy* is universal. One need not be a Christian to enjoy and learn from *The Divine Comedy*. All of us sin, and probably most of us regret sinning. Many people can identify with the characters of *The Divine Comedy*. For example, Francesca da Rimini refuses to take responsibility for her actions, instead casting blame on other people. Many of us have done exactly the same thing.

Reading *The Divine Comedy* seriously will take some work. Readers will need to know something about Dante's biography, about the history of his time and previous eras, and about literature. However, *The Divine Comedy* is relevant to our lives today, and this book and its companion volumes can be your guide to Dante's *Divine Comedy*.

• **What are some of the really big issues that are of concern to *The Divine Comedy*?**

One big issue is sin. For example, what are the results of sin?

One big issue is spiritual transformation. For example, how can one purge him- or herself of sin?

One big issue is politics. For example, Dante warns the reader about the dangers of extreme factionalism.

One big issue is poetry. How can poetry help us?

Of course, one really big issue is this: How do I enter Paradise?

• **This book can be your guide to *The Inferno*. What is the purpose of a guide?**

A guide will help you to cover territory safely the first time you go through the territory. However, many guides, including teachers, want to make themselves irrelevant. By reading this book as you read Dante's *Inferno*, you will get a good grasp of the material, but I hope that you continue to read *The Divine Comedy* and the *Inferno* on your own, making it a part of your life and going beyond what is written here. *The Divine Comedy* is one of the Great

Books of Western Literature — a book that you can reread with interest and profit each year of your life.

• Briefly, what are the major facts of the biography of Dante the Poet?

Dante was born in 1265 in Florence, Italy. He was successful in both poetry and politics. Early, he fell in love with Beatrice, a woman who died young in 1290. Both Dante and Beatrice married other people. About Beatrice Dante wrote a group of poems that he published in a volume (with commentary) titled *Vita Nuova* (*The New Life*).

Dante was a member of the political group known as the Guelfs, but when the Guelfs split into rival factions, he became a White Guelf. The White Guelfs opposed the Pope and wanted Florence to be free from papal power, while the Black Guelfs supported the Pope and were willing to do his bidding if he put them in power. Not surprisingly, Pope Boniface VIII supported the Black Guelfs, and he sent troops to Florence who took over the city in November of 1301. We can date Dante's exile from Florence at this time, but he was officially exiled in January of 1302. Dante never returned to Florence.

While in exile, Dante composed his masterpiece: *The Divine Comedy*. He died on Ravenna in 1321 at age 56.

By the way, "Guelf" is sometimes spelled "Guelph."

• What does the title *The Divine Comedy* mean?

Dante called his poem the *Commedia* or *Comedy*. In the 16th century, the word *Divina* or *Divine* was added to the title to show that it was a work rooted in religion.

The Divine Comedy is a "comedy" for two reasons:

1) *The Divine Comedy* was not written in Latin, but was instead written in the "vulgar" language of Italian. Being written in a "vulgar" language, the vernacular, it is written in a language that was regarded as not suited for tragedy.

2) The epic poem has a happy ending.

• What is the difference between Dante the Pilgrim and Dante the Poet?

Dante the Pilgrim is different from Dante the Poet. Dante the Pilgrim is a character in *The Divine Comedy*. At the beginning, he is naive and sometimes believes the spin that the sinners in the *Inferno* put on their own stories. However, Dante the Poet is an older, wiser Dante. Dante the Poet has journeyed throughout the Inferno, Purgatory, and Paradise, and he sees through the stories that the sinners tell in the *Inferno*.

Dante the Poet is the author of *The Divine Comedy*, whose major character is Dante the Pilgrim. Dante the Poet has more knowledge and experience than Dante the Pilgrim.

For example, Dante the Poet knows that he has been exiled from Florence because he is in exile when he writes *The Divine Comedy*. Because the poem is set in 1300, and Dante is not officially exiled until 1302, Dante the Pilgrim does not know at the beginning of the poem that he will be exiled. He will hear the prophecies of his upcoming exile that are made in the *Inferno*, but he will not fully understand that he will be exiled until his ancestor, Cacciaguida, clearly tells him that in the *Paradise*.

Dante the Poet is also more intelligent than Dante the Pilgrim. Dante the Pilgrim will sometimes be taken in by the spin that sinners in the *Inferno* put on their stories, but Dante the Poet knows that God does not make mistakes. If a sinner is in the Inferno, Dante the Poet knows that the sinner belongs there.

- ***The Divine Comedy* is an allegory. Define "allegory."**

An allegory has a double meaning. It can be understood on a literal level, but also present is a symbolic level. Literally, Dante the Pilgrim travels through the Inferno, Purgatory, and Paradise. Symbolically, a human soul who will be saved faces trials, overcomes them, and achieves Paradise.

Allegories have many symbols.

- **What do you need to be in the Afterlife in Dante's Inferno?**

You must meet three criteria:

1) You must be dead.

2) You must be dead in 1300 (with a few exceptions where a soul is in the Inferno while a demon occupies the soul's body in the living world).

3) You must be a dead unrepentant sinner. (After all, if you were a dead repentant sinner, you would be found in either Purgatory or Paradise.)

- **What does it mean to repent?**

To repent your sins means to regret them. Of course, this does not mean regretting being caught for doing them, but regretting the sins themselves.

The sinners Dante will meet in the Inferno are unrepentant sinners. The repentant sinners he will meet in Purgatory treat Dante very much differently from the way the unrepentant sinners he meets in the Inferno treat him.

• **What is the geography of Hell? In *The Divine Comedy*, where is Hell located?**

Dante did not think that the world was flat. (Educated people of his time did not think the world was flat.) To get to the Inferno, you go down. The story is that Lucifer rebelled against God, was thrown from Paradise to the Earth, and landed on the point of the earth that is opposite to Jerusalem. His landing made the Southern Hemisphere composed of water as the land rushed under the water to hide from him. In addition, when he fell to the center of the Earth the land he displaced formed the Mountain of Purgatory.

Dante and Virgil will climb down to the center of the Earth, where Lucifer is punished, then they will keep climbing up to the other side of the world, where they will climb Mount Purgatory.

• **Explain the three separate kinds of moral failure: incontinence, violence, and fraud.**

Incontinence

Incontinence is not being able to control yourself. For example, you may not be able to control your sexual desire (lust) or your desire for food and drink (gluttony).

Violence

Violence can be directed against yourself (suicide), against God (blasphemy), or against other people (physical violence).

Fraud

Fraud involves the willful use of misrepresentation to deprive another person of his or her rights. For example, one can claim to be able to foretell the future and charge people money to tell them their "futures."

Simple fraud is fraud, but it is not committed against those to whom one has a special obligation of trust.

Complex fraud is fraud committed against those to whom one has a special obligation of trust. Sinners who commit complex fraud are traitors of various kinds: e.g., traitors to kin/family, traitors to government, traitors to guests, or traitors to God.

• **What kinds of characters will we see in *The Divine Comedy*?**

We will see both real characters and fictional characters. Mythological creatures will often be the guards in the Inferno.

Some of the characters will be important historically and globally, while others will be important only locally and would in fact be forgotten if they had not been mentioned in the *Inferno*.

• What do the sinners in the Inferno all have in common? Why can't we take what the sinners say at face value?

They have in common the fact that they are unrepentant. They do not take responsibility for the sins they have committed. Because of that, they will spin their stories and try to put the blame on someone or something else.

When we read the *Inferno*, we must be careful to try to see the whole story. The sinners will **not** tell the truth, the whole truth, and nothing but the truth. (Reading this retelling of Dante's *Inferno* or the notes in the translation of the *Inferno* that you are reading can help you to understand when a character is trying to spin you.)

Be aware that many people in the *Inferno* are going to be able to tell a good story, and you may end up thinking — like Dante the Pilgrim sometimes — that a certain sinner does not belong in Hell. However, Dante the Poet realizes that God doesn't make mistakes. Anyone who is in Hell deserves to be in Hell. It's important to closely examine the stories of some persuasive sinners to see what they are leaving out.

• Why do people sin?

Two main reasons, perhaps:

1) A lack of will. Often, we know what we ought to do, but we can't bring ourselves to do it. (Everyone who needs to lose 10 pounds knows exactly what to do to lose it: Exercise more and eat less. Someone who exercises less than they should and eats more than they should without a good reason such as illness is guilty of the sin of gluttony.)

2) An attractive veneer. Sometimes, sinning can appear to be attractive and to be fun, and thus people are tempted to sin. (Staying up late, getting drunk, and partying can be fun, but if these things prevent a student from attending class, that student is guilty of the sin of sloth.)

• Does God make mistakes? Do these sinners belong in the Inferno?

We must be careful when reading the *Inferno*. Dante the Pilgrim will sympathize with some sinners early in the *Inferno*, and we may be tempted to do exactly the same thing, but God is omniscient, omnipotent, and omnibenevolent. God does not make mistakes. If a sinner is in the Inferno, the sinner belongs there.

By the way, the difference between *Inferno* and Inferno is that *Inferno* is the title of a book and Inferno is the name of a place. (Similarly, *Hamlet* is the title of a play, and Hamlet is the name of a character in that play.)

Conclusion

Once you have read this retelling in prose of Dante's great epic poem *Inferno*, you will have a good but basic understanding of it.

Then go and read the real thing. I recommend the translation by Mark Musa. The translation by John Ciardi is also very good.

Appendix B: About the Author

It was a dark and stormy night. Suddenly a cry rang out, and on a hot summer night in 1954, Josephine, wife of Carl Bruce, gave birth to a boy — me. Unfortunately, this young married couple allowed Reuben Saturday, Josephine's brother, to name their first-born. Reuben, aka "The Joker," decided that Bruce was a nice name, so he decided to name me Bruce Bruce. I have gone by my middle name — David — ever since.

Being named Bruce David Bruce hasn't been all bad. Bank tellers remember me very quickly, so I don't often have to show an ID. It can be fun in charades, also. When I was a counselor as a teenager at Camp Echoing Hills in Warsaw, Ohio, a fellow counselor gave the signs for "sounds like" and "two words," then she pointed to a bruise on her leg twice. Bruise Bruise? Oh yeah, Bruce Bruce is the answer!

Uncle Reuben, by the way, gave me a haircut when I was in kindergarten. He cut my hair short and shaved a small bald spot on the back of my head. My mother wouldn't let me go to school until the bald spot grew out again.

Of all my brothers and sisters (six in all), I am the only transplant to Athens, Ohio. I was born in Newark, Ohio, and have lived all around Southeastern Ohio. However, I moved to Athens to go to Ohio University and have never left.

At Ohio U, I never could make up my mind whether to major in English or Philosophy, so I got a bachelor's degree with a double major in both areas, then I added a Master of Arts degree in English and a Master of Arts degree in Philosophy. Yes, I have my MAMA degree.

Currently, and for a long time to come (I eat fruits and veggies), I am spending my retirement writing books such as *Nadia Comaneci: Perfect 10*, *The Funniest People in Dance*, *Homer's* Iliad: *A Retelling in Prose*, and *William Shakespeare's* Othello: *A Retelling in Prose*.

By the way, my sister Brenda Kennedy writes romances such as *A New Beginning* and *Shattered Dreams*.

Appendix C: Some Books by David Bruce

Retellings of a Classic Work of Literature

Arden of Faversham: *A Retelling*

Ben Jonson's The Alchemist: *A Retelling*

Ben Jonson's The Arraignment, or Poetaster: *A Retelling*

Ben Jonson's Bartholomew Fair: *A Retelling*

Ben Jonson's The Case is Altered: *A Retelling*

Ben Jonson's Catiline's Conspiracy: *A Retelling*

Ben Jonson's The Devil is an Ass: *A Retelling*

Ben Jonson's Epicene: *A Retelling*

Ben Jonson's Every Man in His Humor: *A Retelling*

Ben Jonson's Every Man Out of His Humor: *A Retelling*

Ben Jonson's The Fountain of Self-Love, or Cynthia's Revels: *A Retelling*

Ben Jonson's The Magnetic Lady, or Humors Reconciled: *A Retelling*

Ben Jonson's The New Inn, or The Light Heart: *A Retelling*

Ben Jonson's Sejanus' Fall: *A Retelling*

Ben Jonson's The Staple of News: *A Retelling*

Ben Jonson's A Tale of a Tub: *A Retelling*

Ben Jonson's Volpone, or the Fox: *A Retelling*

Christopher Marlowe's Complete Plays: Retellings

Christopher Marlowe's Dido, Queen of Carthage: *A Retelling*

Christopher Marlowe's Doctor Faustus: *Retellings of the 1604 A-Text and of the 1616 B-Text*

Christopher Marlowe's Edward II: *A Retelling*

Christopher Marlowe's The Massacre at Paris: *A Retelling*

Christopher Marlowe's The Rich Jew of Malta: *A Retelling*

Christopher Marlowe's Tamburlaine, Parts 1 and 2: *Retellings*

Dante's Divine Comedy: *A Retelling in Prose*

Dante's Inferno: *A Retelling in Prose*

Dante's Purgatory: *A Retelling in Prose*

Dante's Paradise: *A Retelling in Prose*

The Famous Victories of Henry V: *A Retelling*

From the Iliad *to the* Odyssey: *A Retelling in Prose of Quintus of Smyrna's* Posthomerica

George Chapman, Ben Jonson, and John Marston's Eastward Ho! *A Retelling*

George Peele's The Arraignment of Paris: *A Retelling*

George Peele's The Battle of Alcazar: *A Retelling*

George Peele's David and Bathsheba, and the Tragedy of Absalom: *A Retelling*

George Peele's Edward I: *A Retelling*

George Peele's The Old Wives' Tale: *A Retelling*

George-a-Greene: *A Retelling*

The History of King Leir: A Retelling

Homer's Iliad: *A Retelling in Prose*

Homer's Odyssey: *A Retelling in Prose*

J.W. Gent.'s The Valiant Scot: *A Retelling*

Jason and the Argonauts: A Retelling in Prose of Apollonius of Rhodes' Argonautica

John Ford: Eight Plays Translated into Modern English

John Ford's The Broken Heart: *A Retelling*

John Ford's The Fancies, Chaste and Noble: *A Retelling*

John Ford's The Lady's Trial: *A Retelling*

John Ford's The Lover's Melancholy: *A Retelling*

John Ford's Love's Sacrifice: *A Retelling*

John Ford's Perkin Warbeck: *A Retelling*

John Ford's The Queen: *A Retelling*

John Ford's 'Tis Pity She's a Whore: *A Retelling*

John Lyly's Campaspe: *A Retelling*

John Lyly's Galatea: *A Retelling*

John Lyly's Love's Metamorphosis: *A Retelling*

John Lyly's Midas: *A Retelling*

John Lyly's Sappho and Phao: *A Retelling*

John Webster's The White Devil: *A Retelling*

King Edward III: *A Retelling*

Margaret Cavendish's The Unnatural Tragedy: *A Retelling*

The Merry Devil of Edmonton: *A Retelling*

Robert Greene's Friar Bacon and Friar Bungay: *A Retelling*

The Taming of a Shrew: *A Retelling*

Tarlton's Jests: A Retelling

The Trojan War and Its Aftermath: Four Ancient Epic Poems

Virgil's Aeneid: *A Retelling in Prose*

William Shakespeare's 5 Late Romances: Retellings in Prose

William Shakespeare's 10 Histories: Retellings in Prose

William Shakespeare's 11 Tragedies: Retellings in Prose

William Shakespeare's 12 Comedies: Retellings in Prose

William Shakespeare's 38 Plays: Retellings in Prose

William Shakespeare's 1 Henry IV, aka Henry IV, Part 1: *A Retelling in Prose*

William Shakespeare's 2 Henry IV, aka Henry IV, Part 2: *A Retelling in Prose*

William Shakespeare's 1 Henry VI, aka Henry VI, Part 1: *A Retelling in Prose*

William Shakespeare's 2 Henry VI, aka Henry VI, Part 2: *A Retelling in Prose*

William Shakespeare's 3 Henry VI, aka Henry VI, Part 3: *A Retelling in Prose*

William Shakespeare's All's Well that Ends Well: *A Retelling in Prose*

William Shakespeare's Antony and Cleopatra: *A Retelling in Prose*

William Shakespeare's As You Like It: *A Retelling in Prose*

William Shakespeare's The Comedy of Errors: *A Retelling in Prose*

William Shakespeare's Coriolanus: *A Retelling in Prose*
William Shakespeare's Cymbeline: *A Retelling in Prose*
William Shakespeare's Hamlet: *A Retelling in Prose*
William Shakespeare's Henry V: *A Retelling in Prose*
William Shakespeare's Henry VIII: *A Retelling in Prose*
William Shakespeare's Julius Caesar: *A Retelling in Prose*
William Shakespeare's King John: *A Retelling in Prose*
William Shakespeare's King Lear: *A Retelling in Prose*
William Shakespeare's Love's Labor's Lost: *A Retelling in Prose*
William Shakespeare's Macbeth: *A Retelling in Prose*
William Shakespeare's Measure for Measure: *A Retelling in Prose*
William Shakespeare's The Merchant of Venice: *A Retelling in Prose*
William Shakespeare's The Merry Wives of Windsor: *A Retelling in Prose*
William Shakespeare's A Midsummer Night's Dream: *A Retelling in Prose*
William Shakespeare's Much Ado About Nothing: *A Retelling in Prose*
William Shakespeare's Othello: *A Retelling in Prose*
William Shakespeare's Pericles, Prince of Tyre: *A Retelling in Prose*
William Shakespeare's Richard II: *A Retelling in Prose*
William Shakespeare's Richard III: *A Retelling in Prose*
William Shakespeare's Romeo and Juliet: *A Retelling in Prose*
William Shakespeare's The Taming of the Shrew: *A Retelling in Prose*
William Shakespeare's The Tempest: *A Retelling in Prose*
William Shakespeare's Timon of Athens: *A Retelling in Prose*
William Shakespeare's Titus Andronicus: *A Retelling in Prose*
William Shakespeare's Troilus and Cressida: *A Retelling in Prose*
William Shakespeare's Twelfth Night: *A Retelling in Prose*
William Shakespeare's The Two Gentlemen of Verona: *A Retelling in Prose*
William Shakespeare's The Two Noble Kinsmen: *A Retelling in Prose*
William Shakespeare's The Winter's Tale: *A Retelling in Prose*